The
Accident

Also by Todd Strasser

For Young Readers

ANGEL DUST BLUES
THE COMPLETE COMPUTER POPULARITY PROGRAM
FERRIS BUELLER'S DAY OFF
FRIENDS TILL THE END
THE MALL FROM OUTER SPACE
ROCK 'N' ROLL NIGHTS
TURN IT UP!
A VERY TOUCHY SUBJECT
THE WAVE
WILDLIFE
WORKIN' FOR PEANUTS

For Adults
THE FAMILY MAN

The Accident

TODD STRASSER

Delacorte Press

Published by
Delacorte Press
The Bantam Doubleday Dell Publishing Group, Inc.
666 Fifth Avenue
New York, New York 10103

Library of Congress Cataloging in Publication Data
Strasser, Todd.
The accident/by Todd Strasser.
p.   cm.
Summary: After four of his friends leave a beer party and suffer a
fatal accident, eighteen-year-old Matt senses something peculiar
about the police investigation and suspects a cover-up to hide the
identity of who was really responsible for the accident.
ISBN 0-440-50061-3
[1. Drunk driving—Fiction. 2. Mystery and detective stories.]
I. Title.
PZ7.S899Ac   1988
[Fic]—dc19   87-37411
                                                            CIP
                                                             AC

Manufactured in the United States of America

October 1988
10   9   8   7   6   5   4   3   2   1
BG

To Glen Gilbert

*I would like to thank Olga Litowinsky
for her patient guidance and wisdom.*

Part One

1

"If you go up there, Matt, I'll never talk to you again."

"I just want to try it once," Matt Thompson said. "What's the big deal?"

Karen Shecter put her book down and counted on her fingers. "It's off limits, it's dangerous, and you're not that good a skier."

Matt looked out at the sun deck of the chalet where his friends were finishing the burgers Bobby Stewart had grilled for lunch. Beyond them chair lifts and ski trails stretched up to the snowy peak of Flathead Mountain.

"You're just mad because I said I'd ski with you this afternoon," Matt said. "Let me take this run and then I promise I will."

"Do you know how many times you've said, 'Karen, just let me do this and then I promise . . .' 'Karen, it'll take me five minutes and then I swear . . .' Why should I believe you anymore?"

"Because this time it's really true," Matt said.

Karen rolled her eyes. "Matt, you're—"

The glass door slid open and Bobby came into the kitchen. "Uh-oh, at it again."

Karen's face turned red. She picked up the book and headed out of the kitchen. "I'm going upstairs. If you make it down without killing yourself, I'll look forward to skiing with you."

Matt and Bobby listened to her footsteps on the stairs.

"Sometimes I feel like I'm married," Matt said.

Bobby gave him a dubious look.

"I'm serious," Matt told him. "She got accepted on early admission to Tufts and I'm waiting to hear from BU. She's got it all planned. Another four years guaranteed."

Bobby went to the refrigerator and took out a couple of Coors. "If you don't like it, Matt, I know at least ten guys who'd be glad to take your place."

"Gee, thanks."

Bobby winked at him. "Anytime, pal."

The chalet, which belonged to Bobby's parents, was built right at the foot of Flathead Mountain, so close to the lifts that you could ski to the front door. From the sun deck you could see the whole ski area, including the

4

long cornice of windswept snow Bobby wanted to jump from. The cornice was shaped like a huge curling wave. The idea was you climbed to the top of it, then pushed off and dropped straight down about twenty feet through the air before landing in the steep virgin powder below. According to the trail map the area was off limits, but Bobby said he did it all the time.

After lunch, Bobby, Matt, and Jason Ellman skied over to the triple chair. The two other girls who'd come along for the day, Randy Chapman and Susie Zorn, said they wanted to stay behind on the deck and get some sun.

"It's a rush," Bobby said as they rode the chair up. "For a couple of seconds you're completely airborne. Then you hit the powder and glide through your turns."

"That simple, huh?" Jason sounded dubious. The three of them had skied together that morning. Jason was an intermediate and Matt wasn't much better. Bobby was so smooth and quick that it seemed as if he floated downhill on a cushion of air.

"Don't sweat it," Bobby said. "You guys'll be fine."

The triple chair ended at the tree line and they skied over to another chair lift, which brought them to the top of the mountain. Vast fields of snow surrounded them. Except for the warming hut on the summit there was no protection from the cold and wind. Matt felt his ears sting and zipped his parka up to his chin while he stared at the awesome mountain peaks in the distance. Bobby and Jason were already halfway toward the cornice, and Matt had to ski fast to catch up with them. A few moments later the three of them passed a sign that said, NO SKIING PAST THIS POINT. Beyond it was the cornice. To the right it sloped steeply away into the back country. To the left was a giant lip of snow and then a steep bowl leading down to the regular ski runs. Between the lip and bowl was nothing but air. Matt's mouth felt dry and his heart began to beat hard.

Bobby stopped on top of the cornice. The tips of his skis hung over the edge as he gazed down at the bowl below. Matt and Jason stopped next to him. Jason looked pale.

"I know it looks scary," Bobby said, trying to soothe them. "But it's only fifteen or twenty feet till you hit snow. Like going off the high board at the town pool."

"Sure, I always go off the high board on skis," Jason said with a smirk.

"Just remember, Ace, you can't fall off a mountain. You can fall down it, but not off it."

Jason forced a laugh. "Gee, I feel better already."

Matt felt dizzy. Not only was he supposed to launch himself off the cornice into thin air, but the bowl below was steeper than anything he'd ever skied. And he'd never really mastered powder skiing either.

"Sit back with your weight on your heels and your knees bent," Bobby told them. "The powder absorbs a lot of the impact. Then you can either start your turns or stop."

"How?" Jason asked.

Bobby grinned at him. He probably thought Jason was kidding, but Matt wasn't so sure. "See you at the bottom, guys." He planted his poles and pushed off, dropping out of sight.

Matt and Jason craned their necks to see past the edge of the cornice. A second passed. Matt thought Bobby was out of sight too long. He must have crashed. Maybe he was hurt. . . .

But a moment later Bobby skied into view, slashing

back and forth through the deep powder in the bowl, then coming to a stop about halfway down and looking back up at them. He raised his poles victoriously, then waved for Jason and Matt to follow.

Up on top of the cornice, the wind blew swirls of loose snow around their ankles.

"You first," Jason said.

"No way," said Matt.

Jason tried crouching with his weight back the way Bobby had instructed. Then he straightened up again and leaned on his poles.

"It's crazy," he said, soberly.

"I know," said Matt.

"Better not think about it," Jason said. He planted his poles and slid his skis forward. The next thing Matt knew, he'd pushed off and disappeared.

Matt couldn't believe it. He'd never expected Jason to go. In the back of his mind, he'd pictured them standing on the cornice for a while, then deciding it was insane and hiking back to the summit to ski the regular trails down. But now Jason was gone, and out of sight for much longer than Bobby had been.

A minute passed, then two. The only sound was the wind. Matt leaned as far forward as he dared, straining to see over the edge. Maybe Jason was hurt. But Bobby hadn't moved from his spot, so he waited.

Finally Jason skied into sight, covered from head to foot with snow. He must have fallen. He stopped next to Bobby and they gave each other high fives. Then he turned and looked up at Matt, raising his poles and grinning.

On the cornice, the wind sent chills down Matt's spine. Jason had done it. It didn't matter how. It only mattered that he and Bobby were down there and Matt was still on top.

Matt inched the tips of his skis a little farther over the edge of the cornice. He looked down at the two trails through the snow below. Bobby's was smooth and symmetrical like a snake's. Jason's was jagged like the edge of a broken window. Jason was new at school that year and he seemed determined to replace Matt as Bobby's best friend. Up till then, Matt had felt ambivalent toward him, regarding him as half pest and half competitor. Now he simply hated him.

Bobby and Jason were waving at him. Bobby cupped his hands around his mouth and yelled something, but it was lost in the wind. Matt's heart felt as if it were three sizes too big and pounding three times too hard in his chest. He stared down again and tried to imagine dropping through the void to the snow. *"You're not that good a skier,"* Karen had said. Matt swore to himself. He knew she was right.

If only Jason hadn't done it. Matt swore again, and backed away from the cornice.

"I chickened out," Matt said glumly. It was late afternoon. Up on the mountain the lifts had stopped running. The sun had dropped, leaving the valley in shadows and the peaks aglow with orange-tinted light. Matt and Karen strapped their skis onto the rack on her car. Jason and Susie were still in the chalet. Bobby and Randy were loading Bobby's ZX Turbo for the trip back to Highland Hills.

"You didn't," Karen said.

"Jason did it."

"He could have been killed."

"No," said Matt.

8

"Well, he could have been hurt," Karen said. "There's a difference between bravery and blind stupidity. You're not that good a skier."

Why did she have to keep telling him? Did she really think he didn't know?

Matt picked up her Rossignols and slid them onto the rack. "It'll get around school."

"So let it," Karen said, unconcerned. "You think people are really going to laugh at you because you had the brains not to jump off a cliff?"

Matt shrugged. Maybe she was right, but it didn't make him feel any better. All afternoon, while he'd skied with her, he'd imagined himself back on the cornice. He should have jumped. *"You're not that good a skier."* Maybe not, but he doubted he would have been hurt. He probably would have fallen as Jason had. Then he would've gotten up and skied down to Jason and Bobby. They would've laughed about it. And he'd still be one of the guys, instead of feeling like an outcast.

2

"Did anyone read *The Reporter* today?" Matt's mother asked as she pulled the last steaming Celestial frozen Italian dinner out of the microwave. No one answered her. Matt was pouring water into the glasses. Karen, who often ate over during the week because her parents worked at night, was at the kitchen counter, tossing the salad. Matt's twelve-year-old brother, Peter, had just set the kitchen table with paper plates and silverware. He was now listening to his

Walkman, flicking a fork in one hand and a spoon in the other, playing air-drums.

Holding the hot dinner with threadbare potholders, Mrs. Thompson dashed across the kitchen and dropped it on the table in front of her chair. Karen followed with the plastic bowl filled with salad. A moment later, everyone sat down.

"*Blaacchhh.*" Peter stuck his tongue out and made barfing noises.

"The sound effects are not appreciated," Mrs. Thompson said.

"How come we always eat frozen dinners?" Peter asked. Like a scientist coming across a new form of life, he cautiously prodded the substance on his plate with a fork. "Why can't we have a normal meal once in a while? I mean, look at this *crud.*"

Matt looked at his own dinner, an island of gummy mozzarella floating on a pond of tomato sauce. What lurked under the surface was a mystery.

"I'll bet you anything this is eggplant Parmesan," Peter said. He stuck his fork under the cheese and peeked. "I knew it! Oh, *barfola,* get this away from me!"

He shoved the plate away. The performance was pure Peter. Meanwhile, he weighed eighty pounds and was built like a stick insect.

"Want my spinach lasagna?" Mrs. Thompson asked.

"Ugh. Vomitsville." Peter made his eyes bulge.

Mrs. Thompson sighed and looked at Matt. "What did you get?"

Matt peeked under his cheese. "Manicotti."

"Puke City."

Mrs. Thompson turned to Karen.

"Looks like stuffed shells," Karen said.

"How about that?" Mrs. Thompson asked hopefully.

Peter took his time, then said, "Okay."

He and Karen exchanged dinners and they all started eating. Peter's head bobbed to the heavy metal from his Walkman. It was so loud Matt could hear the drumbeat.

Mrs. Thompson reached across the table and pried an earphone off Peter's ear. "How many times have I asked you not to wear these to the dinner table?"

Peter turned off the tape player and scrunched up his face. *"How many times . . ."* he mimicked.

Matt grinned.

"What's so funny, barf brain?" Peter asked.

"You're such a jerk," Matt told him.

"Look who's talking, groin breath."

Karen choked on her lasagna. "Groin breath?"

Mrs. Thompson cleared her throat. "I seem to recall asking if anyone read the paper today."

"Sure, I read it on the school bus every morning," Peter said. "The kid next to me reads *The Wall Street Journal,* and we always have a stimulating conversation about world politics."

"It is not always necessary to show us how witty you are," said his mother.

Peter made a face. "Well, exxcuuuusse me."

"Don't you ever read the paper?" Mrs. Thompson asked Matt.

Matt shrugged. "The sports section sometimes. Why?"

"It's important," his mother said. "I think you should all make it a rule to read *The Reporter* every day."

"Yeah, sure," Peter said. "And I'll remember to floss my teeth every night and do volunteer work too."

Mrs. Thompson glared at him, but Matt knew there was a glint of truth in the wisecrack. His mother was always proposing rules for self-improvement. Of course Matt and Peter never followed them and Mrs. Thompson usually forgot the next day. The rules usually had to do with things Matt's father had done before he died of cancer ten years ago. Matt vaguely remembered his father reading the paper every morning at the breakfast table.

"What's going on in this state is incredible," Mrs. Thompson said.

"Absolutely," Peter agreed.

Mrs. Thompson squinted at him. "Do you know what I'm talking about?"

"No."

"You mean the head of the state department of transportation admitting that he used a quarter of a million dollars in state funds to build a ski house?" Karen said. "We talked about it in school."

"And today they had a story about voter fraud," Mrs. Thompson said. "They can't prove it, but it appears that Governor Hughes bought thousands of votes in the last election. It seems like the entire state government is corrupt."

"Big deal," said Peter. He had eaten about a quarter of his dinner and was mashing the rest into a thick pink goo.

"People expect politicians to be crooks," Matt said. "My history teacher says any lawyer with half a brain can make four times as much in private practice as he can in politics. So why become a politician unless you're dumb and dishonest?"

"Because money isn't everything," Mrs. Thompson said. She seemed annoyed by her son's answer. "And the fact that you and so many other people expect politicians to be dishonest is a sorry comment on the world we live in."

Peter pointed to the pink goo on his plate. *"This* is a sorry comment on the world we live in."

"You're too old to be playing with your food," Mrs. Thompson snapped. Then to Matt she said, "You really feel that there's nothing wrong with being dishonest?"

"I didn't say that," Matt said defensively. "I just said that it happens so much it doesn't surprise anyone anymore."

Peter raised his hand. "May I be excused from this incredibly boring conversation?"

Mrs. Thompson nodded. Peter slipped the headphones over his ears and turned up the volume. On his way out of the kitchen he stopped in the doorway and played air-guitar. His fingers raced up and down the imaginary fretboard as he gyrated into what looked like a seizure.

"Do you think he's normal?" Mrs. Thompson asked wearily.

Karen nodded. "For a twelve-year-old male."

"What's *that* supposed to mean?" Matt asked.

Karen gave Matt's mother a knowing look. It ticked him off. He didn't know why, but ever since the day they'd gone skiing, a lot of things Karen did and said made him mad. *"You're not that good a skier."* Why couldn't she have a little more faith in him? Why did she always have to think and act like his mother? Didn't she know one mother was enough?

"You don't *always* have to agree with my mother," Matt said later that night as he walked Karen out to the driveway.

14

Karen turned and brushed a few wisps of hair out of her face. "What are you talking about?"

"I'm talking about before. In the house. That discussion about politics. And then when my mother asked if Peter was normal you made that crack about twelve-year-old males."

"But that's exactly what he acts like."

"And when did you become such an expert?" Matt asked contemptuously.

Karen scowled. "What's gotten into you?"

Matt pressed his hands into his pockets. It was a cold January night. Above them stars shimmered in the icy black sky. Karen was wearing a warm down jacket, but Matt had come out in his shirt. He was always going out into the cold for just a moment and then staying until he froze.

"I don't know," he said. "It just bothers me. Always agreeing with my mother. And eating over almost every night. And us going to college back East. It's like you're not my girlfriend anymore. You've become part of my family. Like my sister or something."

Karen stared at him, her mouth slightly open. "Well, fine, I won't eat over anymore. The only reason I did it was because your mom works late and I thought I could help in the kitchen. And who cares where you go to college? I mean, God forbid I should become part of your wonderful family."

She got into her car and rolled down the window. "I think it would be better if we didn't see each other anymore, Matt."

She waited for a second, giving him an opportunity to apologize. But Matt felt frozen. If only I'd jumped off that stupid cornice, he thought.

By now the car was backing down the driveway. Of

15

course she was going to stop, Matt thought. He'd never meant to break up with her, he was just mad. Didn't she understand?

Apparently, she didn't. The taillights disappeared around the corner.

3

Clink. Matt opened one eye. He thought he'd heard something, but maybe not. The pillow was warm under his head. Across the room Michael Jordan looked back at him from a Nike poster. Matt stretched. His right foot slipped out from under the down comforter and recoiled at the chilly air. He'd had a dream in which he'd been up on the cornice again, except it seemed as if it were miles above the snow. And all around him were bleachers filled with kids shouting and cheering. He kept looking for Karen, but she wasn't there. Pretty weird. Matt yawned and looked at the clock on the night table next to his bed. It was 7 A.M. He rolled over and tried to go back to sleep.

Clink! This time he opened both eyes. What was that?

Clunk! The window. Someone was throwing pebbles. Matt slid out of bed and went to the window and pulled it open. The freezing morning air hit his face and he squinted in the sunlight. It was a perfect, clear blue, frigid Friday morning.

Bobby and Jason were standing in the frozen grass below.

"What's up?" Matt asked in a low voice.

"We're going to breakfast," Bobby said.

Matt rubbed his eyes and yawned, his breath a white cloud in the cold air. "Why didn't you use the front door?"

"Because then we'd never get to see your beautiful bare bod," Jason said.

"I wasn't sure you'd want your mom to know," Bobby added.

Matt shrugged. The cold air brought goose bumps up on his arms. He noticed the window had a small nick where it had been hit by a pebble. "Hey, you break this window, you're gonna pay for it."

Jason bent down and picked up a stone the size of a large potato. "You mean, if I throw this rock at your window, it'll break?"

"You got it, Ace."

The next thing Matt knew, Jason wound up and threw the rock. Matt ducked, but he didn't hear the sound of smashing glass. He looked out the window

18

again. Below him, Jason and Bobby were doubled up in laughter.

"Where'd it go?" Matt asked.

"Over the house," Bobby gasped.

Matt's was one of six attached town-house units. He could just see Mrs. Walsh in the unit next to theirs getting dressed in her bedroom and all of a sudden this rock crashes through the skylight and breaks her skull. Typical Jason Ellman stunt.

"Hey, Jason, anyone ever tell you you need brain surgery?"

Bobby straightened up. "Look, you want to go or not? I'm starving."

"Okay, give me a minute." Matt pulled the window closed and left his bedroom. As he crossed the hall toward the bathroom he wondered if he should check where the rock had landed, just to make sure it hadn't broken anything. Aw, the hell with it. If anything was broken, he'd hear about it soon enough. Leave it to Jason, although Matt had to admit that despite plenty of opportunities to rub it in about not jumping off the cornice, Jason hadn't said a thing all week. Neither had Bobby.

He went into the bathroom. The tile floor was icy under his bare feet. He wished his mother would spend a little more on heating oil, but money was tight. The law firm where she worked had recently laid off four paralegals and if things didn't improve she might be the next to go. Maybe she was right. Maybe if it wasn't for those crooked politicians, things wouldn't be so bad. As he stood in front of the mirror brushing his teeth, he reminded himself that he had to fill out financial aid forms for college. There was no way his mother could afford all the tuition.

19

He washed his face and leaned close to the mirror to check out the zit situation. Not bad. Almost as an afterthought, he decided to shave. Like the hair on the rest of his body, the whiskers on his face were blond. There weren't a lot of them, but what there was had to be cut once in a while or he started to look pretty grungy.

The stereo went on in Peter's room. Heavy metal was like air for his brother—he couldn't live without it. He took his Walkman to school every day and wore it in the hall between classes. He was the only kid Matt had ever seen play touch football with earphones on.

Back in his room, Matt dressed. Then he headed downstairs, carrying the athletic bag Karen had given him for Christmas.

His mother was standing at the bottom of the steps wearing a gray jacket and skirt with a white blouse underneath. She almost always wore gray and white, as if they were the official team colors at the law firm. Just lately Matt had started to notice streaks of silver in her light brown hair. Wisps of steam rose from her mug of tea.

"You didn't happen to notice if Peter was up?" she asked.

"The music's on," Matt said. He opened the hall closet.

"That doesn't mean he's up," Mrs. Thompson said. She turned toward the stairs and yelled, *"Peter, it's time to get ready for school."*

Matt reached for his parka. Bobby and Jason were wearing their swim-team jackets, but he'd given his to Karen.

Mrs. Thompson cupped her hands around her mouth. *"Peter, you're going to miss your bus!"*

20

"I'm going out for breakfast," Matt said, zipping up the parka.

His mother pressed her lips together and the wrinkles around her eyes deepened. Matt knew she thought going out for breakfast was a waste of money, but she'd given up fighting with him about it.

"I found an empty six-pack in the backyard this morning," she said.

"Don't look at me," said Matt.

"You think Chris has been drinking in our yard again?"

"How come everyone always blames Chris?" Matt asked. "It could have been anybody."

He could see in her face that she didn't believe him. Chris Walsh from next door was the biggest burnout in school, and was always in trouble for something. But if Chris had committed even half the crimes people accused him of, he'd be serving five consecutive life sentences in the state penitentiary.

Mrs. Thompson turned toward the stairs again and shouted, *"Peter! Get down here this minute! I have to go to work!"*

The kitchen phone started to ring.

Mrs. Thompson stood in the hall and listened to it. It seemed to Matt that she was hoping whoever was calling would change his mind and hang up. Matt wondered if it was Mrs. Walsh calling to say a potato-sized rock had smashed through her skylight. The phone kept ringing.

"I'll never get out of here," his mother muttered. She went down the hall and picked up the receiver. "Oh, hello, Angelica."

Matt's heart raced. It was Mrs. Walsh!

"Yes, he's right here," Mrs. Thompson said.

21

That jerk Ellman, Matt thought. I'll break his skull.

His mother stepped into the hall. "It's Mrs. Walsh."

"I know all about it," Matt said. "Tell her I'm sorry and I'll replace the window."

Mrs. Thompson scowled. "What are you talking about?"

"Isn't her skylight broken?" Matt asked, slightly confused.

"Her kitchen faucet is leaking and she wants to know if you can fix it."

Whew! Matt grinned with relief, then gave his mother a look that said he wanted to eat breakfast, not fix leaks. Mrs. Thompson put her hand over the phone.

"Don't you think that poor woman has enough problems without having to pay a plumber?" she whispered.

"Gimme a break, Mom."

His mother got back on the phone. "Angelica? Matt says he'll be right over." She hung up.

Matt couldn't believe it. "You know I was going out for breakfast."

His mother put her finger to her lips and pointed to the wall. "Shh. She'll hear you."

"I don't give a damn what she hears," Matt shot back angrily. "What am I supposed to tell Bobby?"

"Tell him you'll see him at lunch."

"You did that because you don't want me going out for breakfast," Matt said. "You know, you're a real—"

"Watch your mouth," Mrs. Thompson warned.

"*You* watch it." Matt went out and slammed the door behind him. He walked down the path to the driveway. The cold air stung his skin. There was no smog today and in the distance he could see the snowy mountain peaks rising above the white foothills. Down at the curb, Bobby's ZX Turbo was idling, vapor curling out of the exhaust. Bobby was behind the wheel. Jason was sitting in the passenger seat next to him, the seat Matt usually rode in. Matt walked around to the driver's side and Bobby rolled down the window.

"What's wrong?" Bobby asked.

"I can't go," Matt said. "My mother just volunteered me to fix a leak in Mrs. Walsh's faucet."

"Why can't Chris fix it?" Bobby asked.

"Are you kidding?" Jason said. "Chris would turn it into a bomb."

Bobby laughed and he and Jason gave each other high fives. Matt stood in the cold and watched. "So I'll see you at school later," he said gloomily.

"Enjoy the bus," Jason said with a mocking grin. The ZX screeched as Bobby left rubber down the street. At the corner where the sand had accumulated from the snowplow, Bobby went into a power slide, expertly bringing the car around.

Matt watched the car shoot out of sight. If only Jason hadn't come to school this year. If only Karen had more faith in him. If only he'd jumped off that stupid cornice.

4

Over half the families living in Highland Estates were composed of working mothers and their kids. There were forty-eight town-house units—eight groups of six with walls so thin you could sometimes hear what was going on two houses away. The Thompsons had moved there when Matt was eight, the year after his father died. Mrs. Walsh had already been living next door with Chris, who was Matt's age, and Casey, who'd been an infant at the time. Matt had never gotten a precise answer on the whereabouts of Mr. Walsh. The story was he'd just sort of disappeared one day.

The mothers tended to stick together and help each other out. Without really meaning to, Matt had become the local handyman when it came to simple repairs. Mothers trying to get by on a single income were glad to pay him a third of what a licensed plumber, electrician, or locksmith would charge.

A black Chevy Blazer was parked in the Walshes' driveway. Matt didn't think much about it since everyone knew Mrs. Walsh had boyfriends over now and then. He pushed the doorbell. Like half the doorbells in Highland Estates, it didn't ring. The only thing worse than the plumbing was the electric wiring. He knocked.

Casey Walsh opened the door. She was ten, thin, with stringy blond hair and round dark eyes that burrowed into him.

"Hi," Matt said, stepping into the house. He knew Casey wouldn't answer him. She was learning disabled and had a speech impediment.

"That you, Matty?" Mrs. Walsh called from the kitchen. She was the only person in the world who called him Matty. He'd once asked her to call him Matt, or at least Matthew, but it was like talking to a brick.

As usual, the Walsh household was in seminuked condition. Casey's dolls and toys were scattered all over the place, along with Mrs. Walsh's fashion magazines and clothes. Mrs. Walsh was a manicurist at a beauty shop in town. She did toenails too.

Matt found her leaning over the sink, packing towels around the faucet. She was wearing a long blue terry cloth robe and pink slippers with furry balls on them. A cigarette hung out of the corner of her mouth. With

25

makeup on she tended to look a little like a brunette Dolly Parton. Without makeup she looked even worse.

"Thank God you're here," she said helplessly. "Look at this mess." Water was seeping out from under the towels and dripping onto the floor.

"Take the towels away for a second," Matt said.

Mrs. Walsh pushed the towels onto some dirty dishes in the sink. A small geyser spouted from the hot-water fixture. Matt could tell that it had probably been leaking for months, but Mrs. Walsh had ignored it until the leak got really bad. He opened the cabinet under the sink and turned off the water.

"Got a wrench?" he asked.

Mrs. Walsh opened one of the kitchen drawers. Lying among some knives and skewers was a screwdriver with a broken handle, an old hammer, and a rusty wrench. Matt used the wrench to take off the faucet. The washers were worn to nothing.

"You wouldn't happen to have a couple of washers and an O-ring," Matt said.

Mrs. Walsh tapped a red-laquered fingernail against her teeth and looked spacey. "A what?"

Matt smiled. He should have known better. "I'll be right back."

He went back to his house to get his tool chest from the garage. His mother was just backing her Subaru down the driveway. Peter was in the front seat, listening to his Walkman. He'd missed the bus again.

By the time Matt got his toolbox and returned to the Walshes', Mrs. Walsh had poured herself a cup of coffee and was sitting at the kitchen counter watching an interview show on a small TV. Water from the leak dripped off the counter and onto the floor, but she didn't seem to notice.

"You want a cup, Matty?" she asked, lighting another cigarette.

"No, thanks." Matt took a towel from the sink and dropped it on the puddle on the floor. Then he sorted through a jar of washers in the toolbox, looking for one that would fit. Casey stood in the doorway and watched, holding a tattered Cabbage Patch doll missing an arm.

Matt looked up at the kitchen clock. "Where's Chris?" he asked.

"Oh, God," Mrs. Walsh groaned, as if she'd forgotten all about him. "Casey, go wake up your brother."

Casey turned and left.

Mrs. Walsh took a drag on her cigarette and exhaled. Smoke so early in the day practically made Matt gag.

"I don't know what to do about him," she said. "He came in at four this morning."

Matt fit new washers onto the faucet. Talking about Chris made him feel uncomfortable.

"Did you see the Blazer in the driveway?" Mrs. Walsh asked.

"Umm," Matt grunted, concentrating on his work.

"He just bought it."

Matt stopped and looked up at her.

"Do you have any idea where he got the money?" Mrs. Walsh asked.

"Uh, no," Matt said quickly. Chris was rumored to be one of the biggest dealers at school. If what Mrs. Walsh said about that Chevy Blazer was true, then he was an even bigger dealer than Matt thought.

Mrs. Walsh tapped the ash of her cigarette into the sink. "I wish he was more like you, Matty. You and he used to be such good friends. I always thought you were a good influence on him."

"Ha." He started on the faucet again.

"Don't laugh. I saw your name on the honor roll outside the office. You're on the swimming team. You have lots of friends. Like that boy, what's-his-name, Senator Stewart's son."

"Senator Stewart's nephew," Matt said. "His name's Bobby."

Mrs. Walsh nodded. "And you're always working around here. Where are you going to college next year?"

"BU, I hope."

"In Boston? That's far."

"I want to see a different part of the country," Matt said, not bothering to add that Karen wanted him to see New England in particular.

"Chris won't even graduate from Highland Hills," Mrs. Walsh said wistfully. "The only reason he goes to school is because it's easier than working."

Matt was almost finished. He took out his pipe wrench and started tightening the faucet. Casey came back into the kitchen and stood in the doorway holding her doll.

"Is he up?" Mrs. Walsh asked.

Casey nodded and stared at Matt again as if he were a creature from another planet. What a family, Matt thought.

A few moments later Chris trudged into the kitchen barefoot, wearing a pair of black jeans and no shirt. He was stocky, with a good build. Long black hair fell in layers to his shoulders. He had a tattoo of a skull on his right shoulder and a gold hoop earring in his left ear. His eyes looked puffy and he was smoking a cigarette.

"Hey, dude," he said to Matt.

"Hi, Chris."

Chris went to the coffee machine and poured himself a cup. "Man, am I hung over," he groaned.

Matt couldn't believe Chris'd said that in front of his mother. If *he* ever said that in front of *his mother,* he'd be grounded for a month.

"You were out too late last night," Mrs. Walsh scolded.

Chris put his hands over his ears and winced. "Not so loud, huh?" Then he pulled a bottle of aspirin from a cabinet and washed three tablets down with black coffee.

"How can you possibly get through school on three hours' sleep?" Mrs. Walsh asked.

Chris shrugged. "I'll catch up."

"You mean you'll sleep through all your classes."

"Sure, Mom, whatever you say." Chris yawned and looked at the clock. "Need a ride to school, Matt?"

"Okay." Matt wanted to check out the Blazer.

"Lemme get dressed," Chris said. Still carrying his coffee cup, he sauntered out of the kitchen.

"Remember," Mrs. Walsh called after him, "I'm staying at a friend's house tonight. You have to stay home and look after Casey."

"Sure, Mom," Chris said from the hall.

"I don't want anyone coming over," his mother said.

"I'm just gonna have a few friends," Chris said.

"Well, just a few," Mrs. Walsh said, giving in. "And you better keep the music down. Mr. Wallach keeps complaining that it's too loud."

"Sure, Mom." A door slammed.

Mrs. Walsh sighed. "Sure, Mom. Sure, Mom. That's all he ever says. And then he goes and does exactly what he wants. He has his own money, his own car. What can I do to stop him?"

29

Matt couldn't answer her. He also made his own money and had his own life, but he still listened to his mother. Some of the time, at least.

He turned the water on. The leak was gone. Mrs. Walsh opened her purse and took out a couple of dollars. Matt glanced at Casey and her old doll with the amputated arm.

"It's on me, Mrs. Walsh," he said.

"You sure?"

Matt nodded. "Tell Chris I'll meet him outside."

Matt was waiting by the Blazer when Chris came out of his house, wearing a black leather jacket with an old Bon Jovi T-shirt under it. The cold must have stung him, but all he did was flip up the collar of the jacket. He tossed the keys toward Matt.

"You drive."

"Serious?"

"Yeah, I'm still wasted." Chris tapped the side of his head with his hand. "Can't see straight." He went to the passenger side and got in.

Matt slid into the driver's seat. It was icy. The car was used, but in good shape.

"Went to bed smashed, got up smashed," Chris groaned.

Matt could tell he was proud of that. It was part of that peculiar burnout creed: the more messed up you were, the cooler you were. He turned the key in the ignition and the engine rumbled.

"Sounds good, huh?" Chris said proudly.

Matt revved the engine and it made a deep, throaty hum. Chris must have just had it tuned.

"Give it a couple of seconds and we'll get some heat," Chris said, shivering. He reached to the floor, picked up

30

a cassette, and slipped it into the tape player. Music boomed out of the speakers in the back. Chris turned the volume down, probably because of his hangover.

The Blazer lurched as soon as Matt put it in gear. He backed it slowly out of the driveway. It was far more powerful than his mother's Subaru. Chris sat in the passenger seat, tapping his hand against the dashboard as they rode through Highland Estates, passing the bare trees and dull lawns. Puddles frozen into gray ice dotted the street and along the curb lay bundles of colored wrapping paper and Christmas trees still shimmering with tinsel.

They passed the big gray storage towers of the Hunt Concrete and Gravel Corporation. The parking lot was empty and metal gates were chained shut. The company had recently gone out of business, laying off more than four hundred people, including Karen's mother. Luckily, Mrs. Shecter was able to get a job working nights at the aluminum company. But she told Karen the Hunt Corporation had gone bankrupt because the owners refused to pay kickbacks to the politicians who awarded state building contracts.

"Your mother asked me where you got the money for this," Matt said, gesturing to the car.

Chris stretched and yawned. "Saved for it."

Matt smiled. Chris had never saved a penny in his life.

They stopped at a red light and Chris pulled a cigarette out of his shirt. "Think I'll have a party tonight."

"Thought your mom said you could only have a few friends over," Matt said.

"That's funny, I didn't hear nothin'." Chris lit the cigarette and grinned.

31

5

- -

Matt looked for Karen in the halls. By
lunch he still hadn't seen her and he began to wonder if
she'd ditched for the day.

When he came out of the lunch line, he spotted Jason
sitting by himself at the swimming team's regular table.
Matt had never seen anyone move into a crowd so fast.
Almost from the first day of school Jason had attached
himself to Bobby, joining the same teams Bobby joined,
listening to the same music, wearing the same kind of

clothes. In no time he was sitting at their table, acting as if he'd been in their group for years.

Matt chose a spot across from Jason but several feet away. He put his tray on the table and sat down. Jason glanced at him and nodded.

"Where's Bobby?" Matt asked.

"Schneider wanted to talk to him," Jason said. He bit into a hamburger.

"What about?"

"How do I know?" Jason said, sounding a little annoyed. "Schneider always wants to talk to him. That's why Bobby's the captain of the team."

A swimmer named Don Washington joined them. "Might also have something to do with the fact that he's probably the best swimmer Highland Hills ever had." Don was the only black kid on the team, a tall, lanky guy with broad shoulders who swam relays, the fifty free and hundred butterfly.

Jason's cheeks bulged with hamburger. "You ever think of how unfair it is? The guy's six foot four and looks like a movie star. His uncle's a U.S. senator. He's the richest kid in school and everybody loves him. How can one kid be so lucky?"

"Guess he just picked the right parents," Don said, biting into his own hamburger.

"Look at me," Jason said, pressing a finger into his chest. "I'm five foot eight, I've got zits *and* freckles, and my old man has a candy store. Bobby got a ZX Turbo when he turned seventeen and I got a Mars assortment pack. He goes to Mexico for the weekend while I watch reruns of *Pee-wee's Playhouse.* He lives in a mansion; I live in a house that shakes when you flush the toilet."

Matt and Don laughed.

"What are you laughing at?" Jason asked Don. "What did you get for your birthday?"

"Well, my brother gave me a shirt."

Jason gasped. "A shirt? Unbelievable!"

"You try to do better on a cop's salary," Don said with a chuckle.

Three girls stopped by the table. They were giggling like crazy. Matt pegged them for freshmen because they were all wearing the same clothes—white turtle-necks under blue Oxford shirts, striped jeans, and white aerobics shoes. It wasn't until junior year that you discovered you could dress a little different and not be disowned by your friends.

"Where's Bobby?" one of them asked.

"He's in Hollywood auditioning for *Superman Six*," Jason said.

"Do his parents really have a ski house in the mountains *and* a villa in Acapulco?" the girl asked eagerly.

"Yeah, but you forgot their apartment in New York," Jason said.

The girls looked at each other with exaggerated amazement. "Have you ever been to any of them?"

"I've been to the ski house," Jason said.

"What's it like?"

"Big. Like it's got five or six bedrooms. And it's right at the bottom of the mountain so you can ski to the front door. And it's got this incredible outdoor hot tub made of marble. You can sit in it at night and drink beer and watch the stars."

The girls' eyes went wide.

"Have you been to any of the other places?"

Jason glanced over at Matt. With a trace of resentment in his voice, he said, "Not me, but Matt has. He went to New York in the private jet."

The girls gasped. "He really has a jet?"

"It belongs to his father's company," Matt explained.

"But they use it all the time," Jason added.

"What's the apartment like?" one of the girls asked.

"It was okay," Matt said, purposely playing it down. Actually, it was a spectacular glass-lined penthouse with views of almost the entire city.

"Did you see anyone famous in New York?"

Matt shook his head.

"Didn't Bobby once say Madonna and David Letterman have apartments in his building?" Jason asked.

The girls exchanged incredulous glances. Matt imagined that talking to someone who knew someone whose parents might have ridden in an elevator with Madonna could be pretty heady stuff. One of the girls gave him a skeptical look.

"If he's so rich, how come he goes to this school?" she asked. "Why not some private school back East?"

"His parents wanted him to go to private school," Jason explained. "But he thinks they're too snobby. His brothers go to Exeter."

Just then Bobby arrived, his tray piled high with food. The girls grew quiet, as if a deity had entered their midst. Bobby placed his tray on the table, smiled at the girls, and sat down. They stared as he opened a container of chocolate milk. Bobby drank about half of it and then licked his lips.

"Hi," he said.

The girls started giggling like mad. Finally, one of them worked up the nerve to say, "Hi, Bobby."

"What're your names?" Bobby asked.

The girls giggled some more. Then one said, "Shari."

"Tina."

"Gwen."

35

"Is there anything I can help you with?" Bobby asked, obviously amused.

More giggles. Then Gwen said, "No."

"You just want to stand there and stare at him, right?" Jason said a little nastily.

The girls started to blush and bite their lower lips. If Matt hadn't witnessed it countless times before, he wouldn't have believed it. The girls just stood there staring. Bobby waited patiently, too polite to start eating as long as they were watching him.

"Hey," Don said. "How about letting the guy eat, okay? You can come back and stare at him later."

They giggled a few seconds more and then scampered away.

As soon as they'd left, Bobby dug hungrily into his food. He'd brought a dish of catsup from the food line and now he dunked one of the hamburgers into it.

"Why don't you put the catsup on the burgers while you're in the lunch line?" Jason asked.

"Because then the roll gets soggy," Bobby said. "The trick is to not make contact with catsup until the very last moment." He picked up the burger, dripping with catsup, and took a bite.

Jason started to make gagging noises. "Have a little hamburger with your catsup."

"What if I told you it makes me swim faster?" Bobby said, taking another bite.

"Don't tell Schneider or we'll be eating it by the case," Don said.

"You can't blame him," Bobby said. "All he ever wanted was a winning season."

"As long as we have to swim in the Black Hole he can forget it," Jason said.

Bobby finished the first burger and dipped the sec-

36

ond into the catsup. "I can't wait till next year. Imagine having an Olympic-size pool you can swim in year round without freezing your tail off."

"Just imagine dressing in a locker room that has heat, and hot water in the showers," Matt said.

Bobby looked over at him. "You think UCLA ever swims against BU?"

"Sure, in the NCAAs," Don said.

Bobby turned to him. "You decide yet what you're gonna do next year?"

"State College of Criminology," Don said proudly.

"A cop like his brother," Jason snickered.

"He'll probably end up arresting *you* someday," Bobby teased. "What are you gonna do anyway, Ace?"

"Get a big Harley and cruise around the country for a while," Jason said.

"When did you decide this?"

"I've been thinking about it for a long time," Jason said.

"You better start thinking about college, my friend," Bobby said, suddenly serious. "Even Highland Hills Community College has a deadline."

"No way," Jason said. "I'll learn more about life on the back of a bike than you guys'll ever learn in school. And it won't cost near as much either."

6

After seventh period, the halls were crowded with kids pushing toward their last class of the day. Matt saw Karen and waved, but they were going in opposite directions and she either didn't see him or pretended not to.

He was going into English when he felt a hand close on his arm. He turned around to find Chris with a cigarette stuck behind his ear.

"Comin' tonight?" Chris asked.

"Thinking about it," Matt said. "What time?"

"Anytime after eight. BYOB."

Matt smiled. "So what else is new?"

"I don't believe this," Bobby said with a grimace. School was over, and he and Matt were walking down the hall toward the pool for swim practice. Bobby had a copy of the *Highland High Herald,* the monthly school newspaper, in his hands, opened to the sports page. In big bold letters, the headline read:

HIGHLAND SWIMMERS S(T)INK.

"It's true," Matt said.

"So what?" Bobby asked sharply. "Where does Marvick get off telling everyone in thirty-two-point type?"

Matt stopped at his locker and worked the combination. When he pulled the door open, his team jacket tumbled out. The ring he'd given Karen for her birthday fell out of the pocket and slid across the floor.

Matt picked up the jacket and the ring.

"You guys have a fight?" Bobby asked.

"I guess," Matt answered vaguely.

"What happened?"

Matt shrugged. He wasn't keen on talking about his personal problems. "I said something and she took it the wrong way. Or maybe she took it the right way and I said the wrong thing. I still haven't figured it out."

"You tell her that?" Bobby asked, trying to be helpful.

"Haven't had a chance to."

A door slammed down the hall. Marvin Marvick, the editor of the *Herald,* stepped out of the Print Media room. "Speak of the devil," Bobby said. Then he shouted, "Hey, Marvick!"

Matt could see that Marvin already knew why Bobby was shouting at him. There was a time when the sound of Bobby's voice would have sent Marvin scampering for protection. But that was the old Marvin, a quiet, wimpy kid who hugged the walls in the hall to avoid bumping into people. Then he discovered the school newspaper and blossomed into a wisecracking newspaperman, as if it were his identity all along and he'd just never known it. The new Marvin strolled toward them, taking off his glasses and cleaning them on his shirttail. "What's your problem, Stewart?"

Bobby held up the paper. "This. How come you have to devote so much space to how we lost our last meet?"

"Because it's news," Marvin replied. "You think it's easy to fill up four whole pages every month? My staff is semiliterate. There's nothing to write about. I go nuts trying to come up with stories. I swear, last month I almost called in a bomb scare just so I could report it."

"What about basketball? Or wrestling?" Bobby asked.

"They're doing okay," Marvin said. "That's not big news. But when the swimming team comes in dead last in every event except the three *you* swam in, that's big news."

Bobby glanced at Matt who looked up at the ceiling and whistled.

"And don't forget," Marvin went on. "I asked you last week for an interview about your uncle. You could've said yes."

"There's nothing to say," Bobby said flatly.

"Are you serious?" Marvin asked. "The guy's running

for governor. With this big scandal I probably could've filled up half a page."

Bobby shrugged.

"Look," Marvin offered, "I'll make a deal with you. You give me an interview about your uncle for the next issue and I won't devote so much space to how lousy the swimming team is. And don't worry about what to say. We'll just talk about what a crook Governor Hughes is and how the reforms your uncle is proposing will help education. By the way, you hear the radio this morning? The state legislature is calling for Hughes to resign. Of course he'll never do it, but things are starting to look really bad for him."

"Hey! What kind of junk is this?" They turned and saw Jason coming down the hall, waving a copy of the *Herald*. He went eyeball to eyeball with Marvin. "Why do you have to write stories about how lousy the swimming team is? How come you don't write about how lousy the swimming *pool* is?"

Marvin looked at Matt and Bobby, a puzzled expression on his face. "Where's this guy been?"

"He's new this year," Bobby explained.

Marvin turned to Jason. "Listen, bud, there have been so many stories about that chlorinated cesspool that there's nothing left to say. I'd put almost anything in this paper to fill it up, but if I put in another story about the Black Hole, Principal Burns is gonna chop me up and feed me to the cheerleaders."

"Tell you what," Bobby said. "Suppose I arrange for you to talk to my uncle directly?"

Marvin's jaw dropped. "You think he'd talk to me?"

"Sure," Bobby said. "I'll call him over the weekend. But only if you promise to take it easy on the team from now on."

41

"You got a deal," Marvin said.

Bobby and Marvin shook hands. Then Marvin left to distribute more copies of the paper. Matt, Bobby, and Jason headed toward the pool.

"Nerd," Jason mumbled under his breath.

"Cool out, Ace," Bobby said. "You ever try to put out a newspaper? It ain't easy."

Jason shrugged. Bobby folded his copy of the *Herald* into a glider and floated it down the hallway.

"Anything going on tonight?" he asked.

"Chris Walsh is having a party," Matt said. "BYOB."

"Burnout city," Jason said snidely.

"Well, I figured if nothing better comes up," Matt said. "Look at it this way, it's a cheap date."

"He's got a point, Ace," Bobby said. "You still owe me from skiing."

Jason sighed. "Okay, I'll bring some Bud."

The smell of chlorine grew as they neared the pool. Matt took a deep breath. The last thing he wanted to do was spend two hours swimming laps in ice water. Well, maybe Chris's party would turn out to be decent tonight. Maybe he'd even get Karen to come.

- -

C hris staggered up onto the coffee table in the middle of his living room. He kicked off some empty beer cans, a half-finished bag of Cheetos, and an ashtray, sending candy wrappers and cigarette butts all over the carpet. He started to say something, but no one could hear him over the music.

"Turn it down!" he shouted.

Matt, Jason, and Bobby looked up from the couch where they were sitting with Randy and Susie. About

43

twenty people were in the room, all drinking beer. Matt was feeling a buzz. He wasn't sure he'd ever drunk so much in one night. Someone turned the stereo down.

Chris held up a bottle of Lone Star and announced, "I'd rather have a bottle in front of me than a frontal lobotomy."

A couple of people clapped. Someone whistled.

"I gotta show you something else," Chris said, swaying slightly. He finished the Lone Star and tossed the bottle on the floor. "Gimme a new beer."

Someone gave him a can of Bud. Chris was so smashed he nearly fell off the coffee table trying to reach for it.

"What's he going to do?" Randy whispered.

"Probably break his neck," said Susie.

Chris held the can up unsteadily. "Okay," he said. "Who wants to bet I can chug this in four seconds?"

"Impossible," Bobby said.

"Put your money where your mouth is," Chris told him.

Bobby stood up and reached into his pocket. He pulled out a five-dollar bill and tossed it on the table. "You're on."

Chris looked around. "Anyone else?"

Jason turned to Matt. "You in?"

Matt shook his head. He wasn't feeling well. Jason stood up and imitated Bobby, throwing in five dollars he couldn't afford to lose.

"Anyone else?" While Chris looked for bettors, Bobby leaned toward Matt and the others.

"Feel like going up to the ski house after this?" he said in a low voice. "We could get there by midnight, get in the hot tub, and watch the stars."

44

"Let's do it," Jason said. He got up and went toward the bathroom.

Bobby turned to the girls. "What do you think?"

The girls gave each other quizzical looks. Randy was the best-looking girl in the eleventh grade. She'd just started going out with Bobby a few weeks before. Susie was her best friend. Randy leaned toward her and spoke in a low voice Matt could just hear.

"Want to?"

"Not really," Susie whispered back unenthusiastically.

"Oh, come on, it'll be fun."

"For you," Susie said.

"Jason's not so bad."

"Give me a break." Susie groaned.

"*Please?*" Randy begged.

Susie gave in. "Oh, all right."

"How about you, Matt?" Bobby asked.

Matt shrugged. He was starting to feel queasy, and wasn't really in a partying mood anyway. He'd called Karen before and their conversation had left him pretty bummed.

"What's all that noise?" she'd asked.

"We're at Chris Walsh's," Matt had shouted over the music. "Want to come over?"

"Why?"

" 'Cause I'd like to see you."

"I thought you said you'd seen too much of me."

"That's not what I meant."

"Sure sounded like it."

"Look," he'd said, "maybe I was wrong, okay? And what was that stuff about ignoring me in the hall and giving back my jacket and ring?"

"You can't figure it out?"

45

Todd Strasser

"Why don't you just come over so we can talk?"

"Is everyone getting smashed?" she'd asked.

Matt had looked around. Almost everyone had brought a six-pack or two. The refrigerator was filled to capacity, with extra six-packs stacked on the floor beside it. "Well, sort of."

He'd heard her sigh. "I'd rather not, Matt. If you want to talk, call me tomorrow." She'd hung up.

That was when he'd started drinking hard.

Chris got two more guys to lay down bets. Jason came back from the bathroom and started to say something about not being able to get four people in Bobby's car. Before Bobby could answer, Chris said, "Okay, now I gotta find a can opener."

"It's a pop-top, brain," Jason told him.

"Just wait," Chris said. Someone tossed him a can opener and he held the can upside down and punched a hole in the bottom. "Okay, start timing me when I pull the tab."

They watched as he tilted his head back and brought the bottom of the can to his lips. A moment later he pulled the tab and started gulping like a maniac. In almost no time he pulled the can away from his mouth and crushed it in his hand. It was empty.

"I don't believe it!" Randy gasped.

"Four seconds," Susie said, staring at her watch and shaking her head in wonder. "Anyone know the phone number of *The Guinness Book of Records*?"

Chris belched loudly and reached for the money. As he did, he lost his balance and fell to the floor. Everyone laughed. Matt stood up from the couch. He felt dizzy.

"You okay?" Bobby asked, looking concerned.

"Sure," Matt said. "Just gotta use the bathroom."

46

Part Two

8

Jan. 28   FOUR TEENS KILLED IN ACCIDENT
Fifth Survives "Miraculously"
Nephew of Senator among Dead

Highland Hills—Four teenagers, including the
nephew of Senator William Stewart, died early Saturday when a truck they were riding in skidded off a
mountain road and crashed into a ravine.

A fifth teen suffered cuts and bruises when he was

thrown from the truck and landed in a tree. Rescue workers said it was a miracle he survived.

According to police, the Chevy Blazer owned by Christopher Walsh, 18, of 35 Highland Estates, went off Flathead Mountain Road 200 yards north of Route 9 sometime around 12:30 A.M. The truck hit a guardrail and struck several trees before tumbling almost 200 feet into a rocky ravine. Police said the four were killed instantly.

Dead at the scene were Robert Stewart, 18, of Auburn Way; Randy Chapman, 17, of 47 Queen Street; Susan Zorn, 16, of 108 Piermont; and the driver, Walsh.

The sole survivor, Jason Ellman, 18, of 2459 Watkins Bend, was apparently thrown from the truck before it fell into the ravine. He was taken to Highland Hills Hospital were he was listed in satisfactory condition with minor cuts and bruises. A hospital spokesman said he was being treated for shock.

Sunday was a dull gray day. A thick layer of clouds hung in the sky and the temperature was just a few degrees above freezing. Matt sat on the couch, staring out the window. Karen, sitting a few feet away, watched him. Out in the driveway, Peter was standing with two of his friends, talking and glancing occasionally at the Walshes' unit. He wasn't wearing his Walkman.

Matt took a deep breath and let it out slowly. Both he and Karen could hear his mother in the kitchen, talking in a somber voice on the phone. "He would have been in the truck with them," she was saying. "No, it was just dumb luck. Every time I think about it I go to pieces.

. . . Yes, he's here now. I don't know how I'll ever let him out of my sight again."

Matt glanced at Karen and raised his eyebrows. Since the moment they'd heard the news, whatever disagreements they'd had with each other had automatically been put on hold. Right now they had to be together.

In the driveway, one of Peter's friends lit a cigarette. More than twenty-eight hours had passed since his mother had shaken Matt awake with the news, but he was still in shock. He kept thinking that it was impossible. They couldn't be dead because no one his age could die. The newspaper and radio station had to be wrong. His mother wasn't really on the phone talking about it with a friend. It was just a crazy dream and he was going to wake up from it any second now.

Except that he was awake. And it was true.

A dented black-and-white patrol car pulled into the driveway and Peter and his friends moved onto the lawn. The kid with the cigarette let it fall into the grass. A tall black policeman got out. He spoke for a second to Peter, who pointed at the front door of their unit. The man nodded and started up the path.

"Who's that?" Karen asked.

"Don Washington's brother, Lee," Matt said. "One of my mom's friends called this morning and said the police were sending someone around."

They watched Lee walk up the path toward the front door. He was thin, with a long neck and a hat that seemed too small for his head. Matt knew him as one of the few people who consistently came to swim meets, only to watch the team lose again and again. He tried the doorbell, and when it didn't work he knocked. Matt's mother answered the door. Out on the lawn the

51

kid who'd been smoking plucked his cigarette out of the grass and took a puff.

"Uh, hello, Mrs. Thompson. I'm Officer Washington from traffic investigations." As he spoke he looked past her into the living room at Matt and Karen.

A moment later, Matt's mother led him into the living room. Matt and Karen stood up and Lee extended his hand. The hand was so big Matt's practically disappeared when they shook.

"Hi, Matt," Lee said.

"Hi, Lee," Matt said, a little stiffly. "Or should I call you Officer Washington?"

"Give me a break, Matt."

"This is Karen Shecter," Matt said.

"Hello, Karen."

"Please sit down," Mrs. Thompson said. Lee sat down on the living-room couch, his knees shooting out to the sides.

"Can I get you some coffee?" she asked.

"That would be great, thanks," Lee said. Mrs. Thompson went into the kitchen. Lee clasped his hands in front of him. He looked gravely at Matt, then glanced at Karen.

"Uh, maybe I ought to go," she said.

"Does she have to?" Matt asked.

Before Lee could answer, Karen said, "I really should, Matt. There are some things I have to do at home. I'll just say good-bye to your mom." She went into the kitchen.

Lee turned to Matt. "I'm sorry to have to bother you at a time like this. But whenever there's a traffic fatality we're required to do an investigation. It's usually in everyone's interest to get it done as quickly as possible."

Matt nodded. "I guess Don's heard, huh?"

"He's pretty shook up," Lee said. He took out a pad of lined paper and a pencil and wrote something. The pencil looked like a toothpick in his hand.

"Did you get promoted?" Matt asked. "The last time I saw you, you were doing foot patrol."

"I guess you could call it a promotion," Lee said. "After four years of pounding the pavement I've been rewarded with traffic investigations."

"You mean, if you were white it would be different?" Matt asked.

Lee looked surprised that Matt had put it into words. Then he smiled. "Let's stick to the matter at hand, okay?"

"But it's true? What they say about the police department being racist?"

"Matt! Really." Mrs. Thompson came in carrying a tray with a cup of coffee and some cream and sugar. She put it down on the coffee table, and gave her son a scolding look.

"Let's just say it's not as bad as it used to be," Lee said carefully. "And it's getting better all the time." He put three teaspoons of sugar in the cup and took a sip. Mrs. Thompson sat down in a chair near the couch. Matt thought about his dead friends again. I don't know what this is like, he thought, but it doesn't feel real.

Don's brother looked down at his pad. "From what I've learned so far, you were friends with both Chris Walsh and Bobby Stewart. I'm curious about that. Chris ran with a different crowd. How did you, uh, get together?"

"Well, the jocks and burnouts don't usually hang out together," Matt explained. "But if there's a party and nothing else is going on, they'll mix. Chris and I were

53

good friends when we were younger. It's just the last couple of years that we haven't been so close."

"Why?"

"Because he got into being a burnout and I got into being a jock," Matt said. "We just went different ways."

"And the party Friday night?"

"We stopped in around nine to take a look. It was going pretty good so we stayed."

Lee scribbled something on the pad and then looked up again. "The police department has suspected for a long time that Chris Walsh was a dealer. Did he supply the jocks with drugs?"

Matt stared at him uncertainly. "None of my friends are into drugs."

"What about drinking?"

"Everyone drinks," Matt said with a shrug.

"Do you remember what people were drinking at the party?"

"Beer."

"Anything else?"

"Not that I recall," Matt said.

"No drugs?"

"I didn't see any," Matt said.

"But there could have been some?"

Matt shrugged again.

Lee took another sip of coffee and turned over a page of notes. "Considering the fact that you were friends with both Bobby and Chris, can you tell me why didn't you go with them when they left the party?"

Matt had been waiting for that one. It was the first question his mother had asked, and the last question he wanted to answer.

"I didn't really feel like it," Matt said.

"Why not?"

54

"I just didn't."

"Did you suspect they were intoxicated?" Lee asked.

"Well, I knew, actually."

Lee gave him a puzzled look. Matt glanced at his mother. "Is this gonna get into the newspapers or anything?"

Lee shook his head. "It's confidential."

"I was in the bathroom, barfing," Matt said. He felt a little humiliated.

The room became silent. It was Lee's turn to glance at Matt's mother.

"He'd just had a fight with his girlfriend," Mrs. Thompson explained.

"Jeez, Mom . . ." Matt shook his head at her.

"Was it customary for you and your friends to drink so much that you, uh, barfed?" Don's brother asked.

"Some guys do it a lot, but it was my first time," Matt said.

Lee turned to Mrs. Thompson. "If it's any consolation, ma'am, I did my share of barfing in high school too."

Matt's mother nodded. "I imagine it's a male rite of passage."

The officer looked back at Matt. "Do you know why they were headed up Flathead Mountain?"

"Bobby's parents have a ski house," Matt said. "It's got a great hot tub. Sometimes we go up at night and just sit in it and look at the stars."

Lee scribbled on his pad. "Another thing I've had trouble understanding is why Chris would leave his own party. From what I gather there were at least half a dozen people still in the house when he left."

"Chris didn't care," Matt said. "If he felt like leaving he'd just go. He used to leave school all the time."

Lee looked at his watch. "I appreciate your candor, Matt. That's all the questions I have. The last thing I'd like you to do is read a list of people who were at the party. If you can think of anyone else who was there but isn't on the list, I'd like you to tell me."

He read the list. Matt couldn't think of anyone who wasn't on it. Lee took one last sip of coffee and stood up. "Well, that's about it," he said. "Sorry to be abrupt, but I've got a bunch more people to talk to."

Matt and his mother stood up and followed him to the door.

"If you feel like giving Don a call," Lee said, "I know he'd be glad to talk."

Matt nodded, but he knew he'd wait until he saw Don at school. "There's something else."

Lee stopped. "What?"

"All Chris's life he was blamed for everything bad that happened. I mean, if someone's window was broken or a radio was stolen from a car, people automatically said he did it. All I'm saying is, I know this was his fault and everything, but—"

"How do you know that?" Lee cut in.

Matt was surprised. "Well, I just assumed."

"Don't assume, Matt. You may be right, but don't assume."

9

Jan. 29   ALCOHOL CITED IN TEEN DEATHS
Heavy Drinking Reported Before Accident
Town Mourns Loss

Highland Hills residents mourned the deaths of
four teenagers today while preliminary investigations indicated that they may have been drinking at a
party shortly before the accident. But police stressed

57

that they will wait for the coroner's report before deciding what caused Christopher Walsh's truck to crash into a ravine early Saturday morning.

The accident's sole survivor, Jason Ellman, is being treated for shock at Highland Hills Hospital. Police hope to interview him later today.

Classes at Highland High School, where all four teens were enrolled, were suspended for several hours this morning, according to Principal Philip Burns. Students were encouraged to stay in their homerooms and discuss their feelings. The school's guidance counselors and psychologist will also be available to speak to students "for as long as necessary," Mr. Burns said.

Flags around town were lowered to half mast today. A number of local businesses remained closed.

Neighbors of Walsh said that they heard the sounds of a party late Friday night at his home in Highland Estates. At least one neighbor, Paul Wallach, reported witnessing drunken behavior in front of the house shortly after midnight.

Mr. Wallach said that he had complained several times before about loud parties and music coming from the Walsh residence. Police said it was not clear whether any adults were at home at the Walsh residence Friday night.

Senator William Stewart, uncle of Robert Stewart, one of the dead teens, said today that the accident was "horrible and unnecessary." He added that charges should be brought against those responsible for allowing the teens access to liquor. Senator Stewart is running for governor this fall on a platform calling for a variety of reforms including tougher drug and alcohol abuse laws in the state. . . .

THE ACCIDENT

* * *

Matt drifted through his afternoon classes wondering why he had bothered to come to school at all. Every time he went into the hall, girls were crying and guys were huddled in small groups, looking bummed out. Because Matt was Bobby's best friend, people kept coming up to him and telling him how sorry they were. Everyone talked about what a tragedy it was that Bobby and the two girls were dead. No one said anything about Chris. In English, Mr. Dunn read a poem by e.e. cummings about Buffalo Bill:

> Jesus
> he was a handsome man
> and what i want to know is
> how do you like your blueeyed boy
> Mister Death

After he read it Mr. Dunn got so choked up he had to leave the room. Matt alternated between numbness and being on the verge of tears. He'd bite his lip or pinch himself just to make sure it wasn't a nightmare. More than anything he wished someone would wake him up and tell him it wasn't true.

Coach Schneider canceled swim practice, and Matt took the regular bus home. Kids stared at him. He could hardly remember the last time he'd taken the bus. Even on days when there wasn't swim practice, Bobby had always driven him back to Highland Estates after school.

At home, he lay on his bed and stared at the ceiling, the door locked to stop his mother from coming in and seeing the intermittent tears. Another day had passed and the tragedy was still real. He couldn't believe they were really gone. One moment from the party played over and over in his mind—how Susie hadn't wanted to go, but Randy had persuaded her. One less beer and *he* would have gone too.

He tried to imagine death, but couldn't. He'd never been able to picture what happened to the soul. Belief in Heaven, Santa Claus, and the Tooth Fairy had deserted him around age eight. But he couldn't accept the idea of an afterlife of plain, cold nothingness either.

The phone rang. Matt let it ring for a long time. When it didn't stop he went into his mother's bedroom and answered it. "Hello?"

"Matt? This is Lee Washington."

"Oh, uh, hi."

"You okay? You don't sound well."

Matt quickly caught himself. "No, I'm fine. What's up?"

"Listen, I'm sorry to bother you again, but the night of the party . . . I know you were in the bathroom being sick, but do you have any recollection of seeing the Blazer leave Chris's house?"

"No."

"Do you recall hearing anyone mention it?"

Matt tried to recall. "All I remember is someone knocking on the bathroom door and saying something about going up to the mountains. I don't even know who said it."

Lee was quiet for a moment. Matt thought he heard him mutter something to himself. "If I read the list of kids who were at the party one more time, would you try real hard to remember if there's anyone I missed?"

"Okay."

Lee read the list. Once again, Matt went over in his

60

mind who was at the party. "That's everyone I remember."

"Okay, thanks anyway." Lee sounded disappointed.

"Hey, wait," Matt said. "Why did you want to know if I saw them leave?"

"It's, uh, just part of the investigation," Lee said, suddenly sounding evasive.

"But you know they left," Matt said.

Lee was slow to answer, saying, "I can't go into it, Matt."

"What about Jason?" Matt asked, trying to be helpful. "Did you ask him? He must know."

"I'm sorry, Matt. I can't go into it."

Matt was confused. Why did it matter if no one saw them leave the party? And why was Lee being so secretive about it?

"Listen," Lee said uneasily. "Let's just forget about this, okay? It really doesn't matter."

"Uh, sure, okay."

"Take care, Matt." Lee hung up.

Matt put the receiver down. It didn't make sense. First the guy calls up and asks a strange question. Then he gets vague and says it really doesn't matter. What was going on?

10

Jan. 30   TEENS WERE DRUNK—CORONER
Alcohol Found in Blood Samples
Criminal Charges Considered

All the teens killed in the Flathead Mountain crash
last Saturday had alcohol in their blood, according to
the county coroner. Police have still not made an
official announcement on the cause of the accident,
but sources in the department say it was definitely
alcohol-related.

Sources also said that the police are considering bringing criminal charges against Angelica Walsh, the mother of Christopher Walsh, the owner of the truck. Before the crash a drinking party took place at her residence, although Mrs. Walsh was not home at the time.

"It's the same old story," said a source who asked not to be identified. "The parents went out and the kids had a party and got drunk. They decided to go for a ride. The driver lost control and the next thing you know you've got a tragedy."

Meanwhile, funeral arrangements have been announced for the dead teens. A mass for Robert Stewart will be held at 10 A.M. at the Grace Church on Saturday, followed by burial at Highland Cemetery. A service for Christopher Walsh will be held at 1 P.M. at the Franklin Funeral Home on East Avenue. A mass for Randy Chapman will be held . . .

As Matt stepped onto the cold, wet concrete around the Black Hole, the familiar smell of chlorine seeped into his sinuses. The damp, low-ceilinged room was dim. Over the years moisture and chlorine had eaten into the wiring, and only half the overhead lights worked. The pool itself was so small it was a joke. Twenty yards. You spent more time turning than swimming. Matt shivered and sat down on the old wooden bleacher, pulling a towel around his shoulders. Even though practice had not begun, a couple of guys were already in the water doing laps. Swimming was the only way to keep warm.

Don came in and sat down next to him.

"Yo, man."

"Hey, Don," Matt replied gloomily. They clasped hands for a moment.

"How you doing?" Don asked.

"Crappy. How about you?"

"Bummed. Truly bummed." They both stared at the choppy green water, stirred up by the swimmers. Don shivered and pulled his towel around his dark shoulders. "It's so hard to believe, man. I was putting on my Speedo in the locker room just now and I kept expecting to see Bobby walk through the door, whistling like he always does."

Matt leaned forward and put his elbows on his knees. Don was right. Each day was filled with a dozen moments when he was accustomed to seeing Bobby. Suddenly the days seemed empty.

"And they expect us to go talk to that psychologist Miss Duncan in the guidance office," Don said with a trace of disgust. "Like I got anything to say to her."

"I know, it's dumb," Matt said.

They watched the swimmers splash through the water.

"Heard my brother was over to see you," Don said.

"Yeah."

"Barf city, huh?"

Matt smirked. "Lay off."

"You talk to Jason yet?" Don asked.

"No."

"My brother says he's not talking."

Matt scowled. "What do you mean?"

In a low voice, Don said, "Something's going on. The mayor's into it, and a couple of those city council dudes."

"Lee said that?" Matt asked, surprised.

64

Don straightened up. "Uh, let's just say I heard it from an informed source, okay?"

Before Matt could ask him anything more, the rest of the team came in, followed by Coach Schneider. He was carrying a cardboard shoe box, which he put down on the bench. He opened it and took out a strip of black fabric.

"You'll wear these bands in memory of Bobby," he said. "Take as many as you need and get your mothers or someone to sew them into the left seams of your trunks. You can put one on the left arm of your team jackets too. Any questions?"

Schneider looked around. He was a short, broad-shouldered man with a big square head and little ears. He almost always wore a tweed jacket with a beige crew-neck sweater underneath and he almost always looked angry. "Starting right now, anyone on this team who drinks will be automatically cut. If I hear you've had so much as a sip of beer, don't bother to show up for practice again. Don't even try to explain. You're off the team and that's it. Understand?"

The team members glanced at each other furtively. Matt knew from past experience that Schneider's bite was every bit as bad as his bark.

The coach glowered at them. "My friends in the police department tell me Chris Walsh was a drug dealer. But I'll bet every single one of you already knew that. Did it ever occur to any of you to go to the police and help nail him? Of course not. You're all too cool for that. Or maybe some of you even bought drugs from him. Well, if just one of you had had the guts to go to the police, Bobby and those two girls might still be alive. Think about that while you do your laps today. You'll have plenty of time because you're each going to give me an extra twenty to make up for the practice we missed yesterday."

A junior named Shane Stone raised his hand. "You think it's right to squeal, coach?"

Schneider pointed a stubby finger at him. "Thirty extra laps for you, Stone."

"You serious?"

"Try me, Stone," Schneider threatened. "Just try me." Then he turned and left the pool.

11

Feb. 1 BOOZE CAUSED ACCIDENT—POLICE
Criminal Charges Dropped
Survivor Leaves Hospital

Police today said drunk driving was the cause of
the Flathead Mountain accident which killed four
youths last Saturday.

Chief Floyd Simpson said that after a thorough investigation his department has determined that

Christopher Walsh, the truck's owner, was driving while intoxicated. He also announced that he had decided not to press charges against Angelica Walsh, the dead man's mother.

"She has suffered enough," the police chief said.

Meanwhile, Jason Ellman, the sole survivor of the accident, was released from Highland Hills Hospital. Mr. Ellman declined requests for an interview.

When asked why it took six days to determine the cause of the accident, Chief Simpson said, "This was a very serious situation. We had four deaths and the only witness was suffering from shock and may have been under the influence of alcohol himself at the time of the accident. The most obvious causes are not always the right ones and we wanted to make sure we were right."

After swim practice on Friday, Matt walked into town. It was dark and windy and pages from a newspaper swirled in the street. Matt's damp hair froze stiff in the cold air. His stomach felt empty, but after being submerged in pool water for two hours he had no appetite.

A number of people were out on the sidewalks, shopping and coming home from work. They went ahead with their lives as if the tragedy, not yet a week old, didn't bother them. It didn't seem right to Matt. Four kids were dead. Even if you didn't know them, you had to feel something. *How can you shop?* he wanted to scream at a woman coming out of Unique Boutique carrying bundles. Maybe it wasn't her fault. It was just that, unlike her, he couldn't go back to his old life. A big part of it named Bobby Stewart wasn't there anymore.

He stopped in front of the Highland Hills Police Department, a concrete building with columns in front. The cornerstone said it was built in 1968, but it looked much older, as if the architect had designed it that way. Matt climbed the steps and went inside. A woman police officer sat at a desk behind a Plexiglas shield. "Can I help you?" she asked.

Matt touched the thick plastic with his fingers, wondering what the police needed such protection from. "Is Officer Washington here?"

"On the second floor," the woman said. She pointed to Matt's left. "Go up the stairs and through the door marked Detectives."

Matt followed her directions. At the top of the stairs he pushed open a metal door. Inside was a large, open room with half a dozen desks. Only two were occupied. At one, a thin man with black hair and a mustache looked at him curiously.

"I'm looking for Officer Washington," Matt said.

At the mention of Washington's name, the other detective, a heavy, sandy-haired man, looked up. The two detectives glanced at each other. Then the sandy-haired man yelled, "Hey, Washington, you got a visitor."

A door opened at the other end of the room and Lee stuck his head out. He smiled and waved. "Come on in."

Matt crossed the room, aware that the two detectives were watching him. Lee's office had just enough room for a desk and a couple of chairs. A small window faced the brick wall of the courthouse next door. Matt felt a chill and realized there was no radiator or heat duct.

Everything on Lee's desk was in order. The pens and pencils were lined up, folders were stacked with precision. The books in the bookcase were in a straight line.

69

A Norman Rockwell print was hung squarely in the middle of the wall.

"I didn't know you were a detective," Matt said.

"I'm not. This is where they've decided to stick the officer in charge of traffic investigations." Lee sat down behind his desk and Matt sat in the wooden chair beside it. Matt noticed an athletic bag and a basketball in the corner. "So, Matt, don't tell me you've suddenly remembered something."

Matt shook his head.

"Then what brings you down here?"

Matt took a deep breath. "Something's bothering me, Lee."

"Oh?"

"I heard there was a problem with the accident. Something to do with why it took so long to make the official announcement."

Lee leaned back in his chair and studied him. "Who'd you hear this from?"

"A friend of my mother's," Matt lied.

Don's brother gazed steadily at him. Matt couldn't tell if he believed him. "What else did this person tell you?"

"That the mayor was involved."

Lee's eyebrows rose. Matt wondered if he'd hit on something. Lee cleared his throat. "And what's your concern, Matt?"

"I guess it reminded me of your phone call and how you wanted to know if anyone saw the Blazer leave Chris's," Matt said. "I just feel like something isn't right. Like we're not getting the whole story."

"I couldn't tell you, Matt," Lee said. "The investigation is closed. Department rules forbid me from discussing it."

"Who can discuss it?" Matt asked.

"The chief of police."

"Is he here?"

Lee laughed. "I don't know if you meant that to be funny, Matt. But honestly, if it's something he didn't tell the newspapers, what makes you think he'd tell you?"

"Then there's no one who'll tell me?" Matt asked, dismayed.

"Why are you so sure there's something wrong?"

"I guess it was the way you sounded on the phone," Matt said. "Like you wished you hadn't called. And you should hear what's going on at school. Everybody's going around talking about what a screw-up Chris was and how it's all his fault. I even heard someone say Bobby was stupid for getting in the Blazer with him. Maybe that's the way it was. But both those guys were my friends and now they're dead and they can't come back and tell their sides of the story. I just feel like if there's more to it, like if there's something people don't know, then they should be told."

Lee blinked and Matt thought his lip quivered for a second.

"And this stuff about the mayor," Matt said. "I mean, I don't have any facts. It's just a feeling."

Lee sat up in his chair and straightened a stack of folders that didn't need straightening. "I don't know what to tell you, Matt. We did our best with the evidence we had. Maybe you shouldn't take feelings too seriously."

Matt could understand why Lee didn't want to break department rules. Four years of foot patrol in the cold was a long time. But he sensed that he'd reached him. Was it something about his eyes? Lee just sat there watching him, and Matt began to wonder. Was there something there? Or was he just imagining it?

71

12

When Matt got home that night, Karen was in the kitchen with his mother.

"Where have you been?" Mrs. Thompson asked.

"I went into town after practice," Matt said, glancing at Karen.

"Oh? Why?"

"Just wanted to," Matt answered evasively.

His mother gave him a skeptical look. Karen picked up the salad bowl and headed toward the kitchen table.

As she passed him, she whispered, "I can leave if you want."

"I'm glad you're here," he whispered back.

Peter came crashing down the stairs and they sat for dinner.

"Did you see the *Reporter* today?" Mrs. Thompson asked as they started to eat. "Four more letters complaining that the criminal charges against Mrs. Walsh shouldn't have been dropped."

"Those don't bother me as much as the ones that say the other parents ought to sue her," Karen said. "How can those people actually put their names on them?"

"Why shouldn't they?" Matt asked. "They think they're right."

"It just seems so futile," Karen said.

Peter stood up. "I'm gonna eat in my room."

They watched him pick up his plate and glass, and leave.

"How come you let him go?" Matt asked his mother.

"Before dinner he asked if he could leave if we started talking about the accident," Mrs. Thompson said. "I didn't ask why, but he's sat through it for six nights so I said yes. I think it upsets him."

"The accident?"

"The way people are reacting. He's heard some of the things they're saying in town. I think it's hard for him to understand the fury this thing has caused."

"It's incredible how mean people can be," Karen said.

"And it's not just the accident," Mrs. Thompson said. "It's the financial hardships everyone's facing—the layoffs and unemployment, even the anger over these state scandals. So much of it is beyond their control. It's

73

so much easier to take out their frustrations on the Walshes."

Peter called from the stairs: "Mom, could you come here for a moment?"

"What's with him?" Matt asked.

"I don't know," Mrs. Thompson said, getting up. She went upstairs, leaving Karen and Matt alone in the kitchen.

They had seen each other, or spoken on the phone, every day since the accident. The previous weekend, after they'd first heard about it, Karen had spent almost all of Saturday and Sunday at Matt's house.

"You've been really great," Matt said.

"I couldn't let you go through this alone," Karen replied. "Even if I am too much like a part of your family."

Matt smirked.

"I am wondering where I stand," Karen said.

"Well, actually, you're sitting."

Karen sighed. "Matt . . ."

He leaned his chair back and looked up at the ceiling. "I don't know, Karen. Ever since the accident it's been really hard to figure out how I feel . . . I mean, about anything."

"And I'm just supposed to sit around and wait?"

"Doesn't it bother you?"

"What?" Karen asked. "The accident? Of course it does, but—"

Matt slid forward. "Listen," he said, speaking in a low voice, "suppose I told you something weird was going on."

Karen frowned.

"I'm serious," Matt said. "It isn't adding up right.

Little things that don't make sense. Things that Don's brother said."

"That's what you were doing in town?" Karen asked.

Matt nodded. "For all I know, it's my imagination, but I don't think so. And I want you to keep your ears open."

Karen looked at him as if he were crazy, but before she could say anything, Matt put his fingers to his lips. They heard Mrs. Thompson coming down the stairs. A moment later she stepped into the kitchen, a perplexed look on her face.

"Peter just asked me when we were going to stop talking about the accident," she said, sitting down again.

"What'd you tell him?" Karen asked.

"I told him the truth," Mrs. Thompson said. "That I don't know."

13

"Matt? Matt, wake up." His mother was rocking his shoulder. "Get dressed."

Matt opened his eyes. Mrs. Thompson was standing over him, wearing a black dress. He looked at his alarm clock. It was six forty-five A.M. "Jesus, Mom, it's the middle of the night," he groaned.

"Get up and don't swear at me," Mrs. Thompson said brusquely. "I'm going to wake Peter." She left his room.

Matt stayed in bed. The room was cold and he was

cozy under the covers. He closed his eyes and let his thoughts drift. What day was it? Saturday. The day of the funerals. The pleasant early morning sensations disappeared. Matt opened his eyes again. It was still real. God, it was like waking up to a nightmare.

Across the hall he could heard Peter growl. "Leave me alone."

"Don't give me your lip, young man. Just get dressed."

Matt's mother stuck her head back in his room. "Up, Matt."

"What's going on?" He yawned.

"Get dressed. You'll see."

Matt moaned and got out of bed. He pulled on a cold pair of jeans and shivered his way to the bathroom.

When he got downstairs, his mother was in the hall, pulling her coat out of the closet. "Where're you going?" he asked.

"It's where *we're* going, Matt," she said. "Put on your jacket."

Matt scratched his head. His stomach grumbled. "What about breakfast?"

"It'll have to wait," Mrs. Thompson said, pulling Matt's parka out of the closet and handing it to him. She glanced up the stairs. "I'm going to get Peter. You go out to the garage and get some rakes, a snow shovel, and garbage bags. I'll meet you out front."

She went upstairs. Matt wondered if she'd gone nuts. Rakes, a snow shovel, and garbage bags?

He went through the kitchen to the garage and got the stuff. Outside, it was another icy gray, overcast morning. The air smelled as if it were going to snow. Then Matt smelled something else, something coming from his right. The Walshes' front lawn was covered

77

with empty cans, crumpled papers, dirty diapers, and other trash.

His mother came out of the house, followed by a sleepy-looking Peter wearing his Walkman.

"Aw, Mom, how come we have to clean it up?" he whined.

"Because today is Chris's funeral and it's bad enough that Mrs. Walsh has to go through that without having to clean up some idiot's garbage," Mrs. Thompson said, taking a rake from Matt and walking toward the Walshes'.

For the next fifteen minutes Matt and his mother raked while Peter used the snow shovel to scoop the junk into the garbage bags. The garbage stank as if it had been sitting around for weeks. Some of it was stuff any normal person would have flushed down a toilet. Several times Matt had to walk down to the curb and take some breaths of fresh air to keep from gagging. He was glad he hadn't had breakfast. As he raked he looked up and saw Casey watching them from her window upstairs. He wondered what she understood, and whether Mrs. Walsh was even aware of what had happened to her lawn. He decided his mother was right. Mrs. Walsh had enough trouble.

When they finished, Mrs. Thompson went back into the house to start breakfast while Matt and Peter sealed the bags and dragged them down to the curb. It was smelly, disgusting, cold work and Matt was glad when they were done. They took the rakes and shovel back to the garage, and then went inside. Mrs. Thompson came out of the kitchen with her sleeves rolled up.

"Thank you, boys," she said. "I'm proud of you."

Matt's hands were stiff and sore from the cold. He went into the bathroom and scrubbed them under lukewarm water. Anything hotter made his hands feel as if they were being scalded. When he got back to the kitchen Peter was sitting at the table, his breakfast untouched. Mrs. Thompson handed Matt a plate of pancakes and sausage. He didn't feel much like eating, either, but he poured syrup on the pancakes and took a bite.

"Who do you think did it?" Peter asked somberly.

Matt shrugged. "Some nut, probably."

Mrs. Thompson sat down at the table with a mug of tea. "It wouldn't surprise me if it was one of Highland Hills' upstanding citizens thinking he was doing his civic duty."

"Come off it, Mom."

His mother pushed a wisp of hair off her forehead. "I'm serious. I just hope it doesn't get worse." She looked at Peter, who was sitting with his head in his hands, staring blankly at the table. "You have to eat something, hon."

The phone rang. Mrs. Thompson stood up and answered it. "Oh, hi, Angelica."

Matt and Peter exchanged uneasy glances.

"Casey told you? No, no, really, it was nothing," Matt's mother said. "The boys were glad to do it. No, I can't imagine who. I'm sure it was just a childish prank. What? Why, of course we're planning to go. Now, take care of yourself. We'll see you later."

Mrs. Thompson hung up.

"What did she say?" Matt asked.

"She called to thank us and ask if we were going to Chris's funeral," his mother said. "Can you imagine? She doesn't even know if anyone's coming."

"How come you told her it was a childish prank?" Peter asked.

79

Mrs. Thompson poured herself some more tea and sat down again. Her brow furrowed. "Would you rather I told her I thought it was just the beginning of her problems?"

14

The streets around Grace Church, where Bobby's funeral mass would be said, were clogged with cars searching for parking spaces. Mrs. Thompson parked four blocks away and then she and Matt and Peter walked. Under his down parka Matt wore a navy blazer and gray slacks.

A crowd of people stood on the steps in front of the church, some talking in hushed voices, others silent, their breaths forming long plumes of vapor in the frigid air.

Just as the Thompsons got there, a black limousine with red, white, and blue government license plates pulled up in front of the church. The driver hopped out and opened the passenger door. A man wearing a black topcoat got out. He was Bobby's uncle, Senator William Stewart. As he helped his wife and children out of the limousine, news photographers moved toward him, their cameras clicking.

The crowd parted to let the senator and his family pass and then followed them into the church. Matt and his mother and brother joined the others slowly climbing the steps.

Just inside the doors, Matt saw the swimming team standing off to the side, looking awkward in ties, jackets, and winter coats. Coach Schneider was there too.

"I thought the team should sit together," the coach said solemnly when he saw Matt.

Matt told his mother and Peter to go ahead and get seats.

"You better not wait too long," Peter said, standing on his toes and looking over the heads of the crowd squeezing into the church. "It looks really mobbed in there."

"Did anyone talk to Ellman?" Coach Schneider asked.

No one answered.

"Washington," Schneider said. "Go look outside and tell me if you see him coming."

Don went out and came back a moment later shaking his head.

"Okay, we'll try to keep a place for him," Schneider said. "Let's go in."

The church was jammed with people in the pews and lining the walls. Hundreds of kids from school were there and a lot of parents too. Past the pews in front, Matt spotted the casket surrounded by yellow roses. Bobby's swim team jacket was draped over the casket, and a big framed picture of him stood next to it. Matt saw Karen waving at him from the middle of the crowd. He waved back, then gestured that he had to sit with the team. Karen nodded. Matt spotted Principal Burns sitting with some of Bobby's teachers. The mayor was there with most of the town councilmen. And there were dozens of people he didn't recognize—important-looking men in suits and well-dressed women—who must have been friends of Bobby's parents.

Matt spotted Bobby's family in the first pew. His father, mother, and two younger brothers who'd been called home from Exeter. Senator Stewart and his family sat down behind them, with Bobby's aunt and some cousins. They were all dressed in black. Bobby's mother was crying softly and clutching a tissue. Mr. Stewart looked gaunt and had dark rings under his eyes. He turned and looked back at the crowd. When he spotted Matt, he said something to a man sitting behind him. The man got up. It was John, Mr. Stewart's driver. He made his way back through the crowd and motioned Matt to meet him in the aisle.

Matt slid past his teammates.

"Mr. Stewart would like to see you at the house later this afternoon," John said. "Around four."

Matt nodded and went back to his seat.

"What was that all about?" Don whispered.

"Bobby's father wants to see me this afternoon," Matt said.

"He say why?" Don asked.

Matt shook his head. He couldn't imagine why himself. In the three years that he and Bobby had been

Todd Strasser

close friends, he'd only met Mr. Stewart half a dozen times, and never for very long. Bobby's father was always busy, always on the phone or just about to get in his limo or jet and go somewhere. Matt had once asked Bobby what his father did, and Bobby said, "He owns companies." He was the only man Matt knew who wore a tie and jacket every day of the week, including weekends.

The church grew quiet when the priest walked out to the pulpit. With his white vestments and slick black hair he looked younger than he probably was. He grasped the sides of the pulpit with his hands and stared out at the crowd as if he were taking attendance. The remaining murmurs stopped.

"I knew Robert Duane Stewart," the priest began in a loud, forceful voice. As he spoke, Matt was surprised to learn that Bobby had been an altar boy and had sung in the choir. He'd never said anything about it, or hinted that he was religious in any way.

"He came from a family that occupies a lofty social position in our community," the priest said. "And yet he never abused that position, and performed even the most humble tasks agreeably. In all, he was a remarkable young man, a young man so full of life and the joy of living that even this morning I find it difficult to believe that he is no longer with us."

The church was so quiet Matt could hear a foot scrape on the floor rows away. He saw Bobby's mother's shoulders tremble and heard her sob. Mr. Stewart put his arm around her. Matt knew that there'd been times when he'd felt jealous of the things Bobby could do because of his wealth. The trips he took to the Caribbean, Europe, and Mexico. His ZX Turbo. The way he never really had to think about money. But today they were all equals. All the money in the world couldn't buy Bobby back, although Matt knew he would give anything if it could.

"The accident is not yet a week old," the priest went on. "But I have already heard a great deal of talk about who is to blame for these tragic deaths. Some people want to blame the boy who was at the wheel of the truck when it went out of control and crashed into the ravine. Some want to blame his mother for allowing her child and others to indulge in alcohol. Still others cast the blame on those who sold these children their liquor. Why, I wonder, have they taken it upon themselves to name a culprit?"

A murmur rippled through the crowd. "There is a danger when we seek out scapegoats to blame," the priest said. "Because when we do this, we avoid the real truth about this tragic accident. And the real truth is that our desire to blame a boy or his mother is nothing more than a futile attempt to remove the focus from each of us who has taken similar chances with our own lives."

Matt felt as if the priest had aimed that comment directly at him. It reminded him again of how close he'd come. The irony was that the only reason he hadn't gone was that he'd been *too drunk* to go.

"The real truth is that we are all to blame for the death of Robert Duane Stewart and his young friends," the priest said. "We are all to blame because those of us who are older have failed to teach the young the dangers of taking unnecessary risks and the dangers of consuming alcohol and drugs. We are all to blame because those of us who are younger have failed to take it upon ourselves to be responsible and learn these lessons. The saddest truth of all is that the only reason we are gathered here today, and the only reason we have stopped to reflect upon these things, is because we have been forced to by this horrible tragedy."

As Matt listened he wondered if the person who had thrown garbage all over the Walshes' front yard was there in the church with them. Maybe his mother was right. Maybe the man or woman who had done it wasn't a total nut, but just someone who was frustrated and angry and had had to express it somehow. Matt could almost understand. You felt this anger and this need to blame someone. Something awful had happened and while part of you wanted to get past it and go on living, another part of you yearned to know what had really happened. A part of you had been hurt and you wanted to take a swing at someone and fight back, but you didn't know whom to hit.

The service ended with a prayer. Behind him, Matt heard the big doors of the church swing open slowly and felt the cold air sweep in. As he stood up, he turned and looked out the doors and saw that snow had begun to fall. The church lawn and the street and the houses beyond it were all covered with a light dusting of white, as if nature were trying to hide the gray reality of winter. Matt touched the polished wood of the pew. What hid the gray reality of death? He wondered if he would ever go a day without thinking about it again.

A few hours later, Matt helped carry Chris Walsh's coffin up a snow-covered hill in a cemetery outside of town. Bobby's burial had been private, for the family only. Don said they were probably worried about crowds. But no one was worried about crowds for Chris's burial. There weren't even enough pallbearers to carry the coffin until Matt and Peter arrived.

THE ACCIDENT

The light snow was still falling, and collected in the seams of Matt's parka. Next to him Mrs. Walsh's fat brother from Spokane struggled to hold up his corner of the coffin. Peter and three men from the funeral home brought up the rear. Besides Mrs. Walsh and Casey, the only other mourners were Matt's mother, the minister, and two women from the beauty salon where Mrs. Walsh worked. Karen had gone to Randy's funeral.

The ground was slippery with new snow and the brass bar on the coffin was icy. Mrs. Walsh was sobbing, and someone kept blowing his nose, loud. Matt's fingers were numb. He tried not to look down at the polished coffin. The thought of Chris's body inside made him queasy.

A snowflake caught on his eyelash, making him blink. The cemetery was bleak and empty. From the sky the little group of mourners must have looked like a mere speck in a field of white, a period on a piece of paper the size of a football field. How many thousands of people had died the same stupid way as Chris, Bobby, Randy, and Susie? Matt wondered. And how many thousands more were yet to die?

They stopped beside the open grave. Matt wished he could let go of the coffin. The bar was still ice cold, as if it were draining his body heat away, as if inside it Chris were still struggling to live, grabbing for life from those around him.

Matt tried to shake the thought from his mind. A backhoe and two men wearing heavy green coats with hoods stood a dozen feet away. One was smoking, the other leaned on a shovel. The backhoe had probably been used to dig the grave and would probably be used to fill it up again after everyone had left. It annoyed Matt that they'd just left it out for everyone to see. It made burying the dead seem like just another job—to be forgotten as soon as the last clods of dirt had dropped in the hole.

Matt was told to put the coffin down. The minister who said the final prayer was nothing like the dynamic young priest who'd presided over Bobby's service. A slight, white-haired man with a quiet voice, he read through the prayer mechanically and called Chris's sister Stacy instead of Casey.

As the minister spoke, Matt studied the faces around the grave. Mrs. Walsh was still sobbing. Her two friends looked sympathetic, but not sad. One of them was chewing gum. Casey was looking back at him. Her lips parted as if she wanted to say something. Poor confused kid, Matt thought.

The men in green coats set the coffin on two wide straps over the open grave. Matt realized they were going to wait until the mourners left before lowering it. He imagined the coffin sinking slowly out of sight into the ground. Like a vault shutting on Chris forever. If Matt hadn't believed that death was real before, he believed it now. Once you were in that hole, there was no way out. This was the end forever for Chris, for Bobby, for the two girls. Their lives had ended in some holes in the cemeteries of Highland Hills. It seemed so little for people who'd meant so much. Matt had fought back the tears at Bobby's service, but he couldn't fight them again. He turned away from the grave and let them fall.

15

Bobby's family owned land and mines all over the state. They leased property to two ski resorts. There was a mountain called Stewart's Peak and a small mining town called Stewartsville. Bobby had told Matt that thanks to a new form of mining called leaching, some of the old gold mines that had lain dormant for decades were back in business. It was a well-known fact that the Stewarts were not only one of the oldest families in the state, but one of the richest too.

Bobby's father ran the family businesses. His uncle was the U.S. senator and Bobby's aunt ran the family's philanthropy. It was her job to give away money to worthy causes. Bobby told Matt a lot of the money was given anonymously, but it was public knowledge that right there in Highland Hills the hospital and civic center had been built with Stewart family funds.

It was still snowing as Matt steered his mother's car off Auburn Way and drove up the winding drive toward the Stewarts' stone mansion with a circular driveway and a fountain in front. Had the architect added turrets to the house, it would have looked like a castle. Matt parked and got out. The snow seemed to absorb all stray sounds. He climbed the steps, but before he could ring the bell, Mr. Stewart's chauffeur opened the door.

"Hi, John," Matt said, wiping his shoes.

"Hello, Matthew," John replied somberly. He looked pale. "Mr. Stewart is waiting for you in the den."

He led Matt through an immense living room lined with portraits of Bobby's ancestors and into the den. The room smelled of wood and polish. Matt had been in it before and knew Mr. Stewart used it as an office. The only light in the room came from a small lamp on the desk and Matt could hardly see Mr. Stewart at the window, staring out into the dusk.

"Matthew Thompson," John announced.

Mr. Stewart nodded. "Thank you, John."

John left, closing the door behind him. Mr. Stewart stepped away from the window. He looked weary. The lines in his face seemed deeper than usual. He was wearing a shirt and a wrinkled jacket, but no tie.

"Have a seat, Matt," he said.

Matt sat in a chair near the desk, but Bobby's father remained standing, his face in the shadows. He was silent for a moment. Matt realized the whole house was deathly quiet.

"I apologize for not being more civil," Mr. Stewart said, his voice shaky. "But this is a difficult time for us."

"I know, Mr. Stewart," Matt said. "I'm really sorry."

"I don't know if Bobby ever told you this, but I had a brother who died in college," Mr. Stewart said. "It was a boating accident. He also had been drinking. The boat he was in struck a towline between a tug and a barge. My brother was thrown overboard."

Bobby's father sighed. "When you think of the advances science has made. The diseases we've conquered—polio, smallpox, TB. And yet we still can't give young people enough good sense to survive."

The memory of Bobby jumping from the cornice flashed through Matt's mind. And Jason following.

Mr. Stewart moved into the light. "You didn't go with them in the truck that night."

"I was sick," Matt said. "In the bathroom."

Mr. Stewart nodded. Matt wondered if he'd always be remembered as the kid who lived because he'd been barfing. Bobby's father pulled the chair out from behind the desk and sat down. They were face to face.

"Matt, I asked you to come up here because I need your help," he said. "You were Bobby's closest friend. You knew his likes and dislikes. I want to build him some kind of memorial, so he won't be forgotten. I've been thinking about it for days and I haven't been able to come up with anything."

"Like a statue?" Matt asked uncertainly.

"No, something useful. Something Highland Hills needs. I thought about a new library, but Bobby just wasn't that kind of kid. Can you think of something?"

Something the town needed, something that was

Bobby, Matt thought. . . . The answer came so fast it surprised him. "A pool," he said.

"But the town has a fine pool," said Mr. Stewart.

"Not for the town, for the school," Matt explained. "The school's pool is the worst. A piece of junk."

"Bobby never told me," Mr. Stewart said, sounding slightly surprised.

"I guess it's something we all thought we had to live with," Matt said.

Mr. Stewart leaned back in the chair. He looked as if a small part of his worries had lifted. "I suppose I would have to speak to the president of the school board. It shouldn't be difficult."

A silent, awkward moment passed while Mr. Stewart thought it over. A memorial for Bobby, Matt thought. One more piece of evidence that he really was gone. One more nail in his coffin.

Mr. Stewart got up and motioned Matt to rise. He stood up, and Bobby's father put his hand on his shoulder and walked him out of the den.

"I know this must be a tremendous blow to you," he said. "You've never known anyone your own age . . . ?"

"No," said Matt.

"I remember what it was like when my brother died," Mr. Stewart said in a voice filled with sadness. "In a way I think it probably saved a few lives. I mean, among those who knew him. We weren't so reckless after that."

"I know what you mean," Matt said grimly. They stopped in the hallway near the front door.

"There's one other thing, Matt," said Mr. Stewart. "Bobby would have wanted you to have something of his to remember him by. Why don't you take a few days and think it over. If there's anything you want, let me know."

"Uh, thanks, Mr. Stewart."

They stopped at the front door and shook hands. "I'm serious," Mr. Stewart said. "Bobby would have wanted that. He was that kind of kid."

Matt went out the door and down the steps to the car. Asking for something of Bobby's made him feel uncomfortable—he didn't want to think of himself as a scavenger picking at the remains of his friend's life. But he supposed he would do it. Not so much for Bobby or himself, but for Mr. Stewart.

After dinner that night, he called Karen.

"What a day," he said when she answered.

"I know."

"How was Randy's funeral?"

"What can I say?" Karen asked. "Is there such a thing as a *good* funeral? It was awful. I couldn't stop crying."

"Yeah. Chris's was bad too." Matt told her about carrying the coffin, and how practically no one came. "It wasn't fair. I kept thinking that Chris doesn't deserve this. He wasn't a mean or bad guy. People are going around saying that Bobby was a great guy. And they're right. But it's wrong for them to say Chris was no good. Maybe he messed up, but he was a human being just like Bobby. I mean, it's not like he got everyone killed on purpose."

"People understand that, Matt."

"You wouldn't know it from what they're saying," Matt said. "You'd think they could show a little respect for the dead."

While he was talking, his mother came in and handed him a white envelope. "I forgot to tell you before," she whispered. "This came today."

Matt scowled and took the envelope from her. All it said was, *Matt Thompson, Confidential* on the front. There was no address, no stamp, no postmark. He asked Karen to hold on for a second and tore the envelope open. Inside was a single sheet of paper, a photocopy of something barely decipherable. Matt held it under the light. It was a report of some kind. Or parts of four different reports photocopied together. In the top left hand corner were the words *Blood Alcohol Concentration.* Beneath it were the names:

Chapman, Randy	.08
Stewart, Robert	.06
Walsh, Christopher	.17
Zorn, Susan	.03

"Karen?" Matt said hastily into the phone. "I gotta get off. You want to do something tomorrow?"

"I would, Matt," she said, "but I haven't done a drop of homework all week and I feel like I really have to study. I'll see you in school Monday, okay?"

"Well, okay." Matt was disappointed, but his attention turned back to the letter. He found his mother in her bedroom, sitting on her bed, watching TV. "Where'd you find this?" he held up the envelope.

"Inside the front door," Mrs. Thompson said. "Someone must have slipped it through the mail slot while we were out. What does it say?"

Matt folded the paper and put it in his pocket. "Nothing."

He went back to his room, took out the paper, and stared at it for a long time. What did it mean? And why would anyone go out of his way to deliver the information to him? Someone must have been trying to tell him something. But who? And what exactly did he want him to know?

16

On Monday morning, Matt met Karen at her locker and showed her the letter.

"Do you know where it came from?" she asked.

"The police or the coroner's office," Matt said. "I mean, who else would know?"

"Maybe someone's playing a trick on you," Karen said. "All they'd need is a typewriter and a Xerox machine."

"Why would anyone want to do that?" Matt asked. Of

all the possibilities, that one had never crossed his mind.

Karen shrugged and glanced at the mirror in her locker. Under it was a photo of Tom Cruise bare chested.

Matt leaned against the locker next to hers, his hands shoved into his pockets. "It doesn't make sense."

Karen closed her locker and faced him. "Matt, are we broken up or not?"

"What are you talking about?"

"Before the accident we'd broken up. Then after the accident it seemed like we were together again. But maybe that was just because of the accident. I want to know where we stand."

Matt grinned. "We stand in the hallway."

"I'm serious," Karen said, irritated that he was making a joke.

"Uh, look, are you going to the assembly this afternoon?" Matt asked evasively.

"What else would I do?" Karen asked, not following his drift. But Matt hardly heard her. He'd just noticed that Jason was down the hall in front of his locker.

"What is it?" Karen asked.

"Uh, nothing," Matt said, distracted by other thoughts. "Catch you at the assembly."

He left her and jogged toward Jason. The bell was going to ring any second now and the hall was starting to clear. Jason had a bandage on his forehead and the skin around his eyes was yellow and purple.

"Hey, how're you feeling?" Matt asked.

Jason gave him a sideways glance. "Not bad."

"We thought you'd be at Bobby's funeral."

"Wasn't up to it," Jason said, pulling a book out of his locker and making no effort to be friendly.

"Think you'll go to practice today?" Matt asked.

"Can't," Jason said. "I have to wait until the bandage comes off. Besides, I don't feel much like swimming right now."

"Know what you mean." Matt felt he was forcing the conversation. Jason kept rummaging through his locker, almost as if he were trying to ignore him. Then the bell rang.

"Well, see you later, okay?" Matt said.

"Sure." Jason didn't even look up.

The word in the halls was that someone from the police department was going to give a lecture on drunk driving. When Matt got to the auditorium, it was full of kids and yet eerily quiet.

Karen waved to him and pointed to the empty seat she was saving. Matt slid down the aisle toward her.

"Do you believe this?" she asked in a low voice as he sat down.

"Weird," Matt said, looking around. It was so quiet you could have heard a pin drop.

"Makes you wonder why they even bother to have an assembly," Karen said.

"Better late than never, I guess," said Matt.

Kids were still coming into the auditorium and looking for seats. Matt put his feet against the seat in front of him.

"Uh-hum." Karen cleared her throat. Matt knew she wanted to continue the conversation they'd started that morning.

"Remember that day we went skiing?" he asked. "And you said I wasn't a good enough skier to go off the cornice with Bobby and Jason?"

"Yes?"

"Why'd you say that?"

Karen scowled. "You mean I was supposed to pretend you were a good skier so I could watch you break your neck?"

Matt sighed. "See? This is what I mean. Listen to us. We're still in high school and we sound like an old married couple."

Karen was quiet for a moment. "Matt, if you're trying to say you want to see other people you should tell me because there are definitely other people who want to see me."

Matt stiffened. "Who?"

"Eddie Simonds, for one."

"He went to Arizona State."

"He still calls," Karen said casually. "And he wants me to come down over Easter vacation."

Before Matt could respond, Principal Burns stepped up to the lectern. "Thank you, ladies and gentlemen, for settling down," he said solemnly. "We've arranged today to have a spokesman from the police department speak to you about drunk driving. Ever since the tragedy a week ago, one thing the guidance counselors and I have noticed is that there seems to be a lot of confusion about the effects of alcohol on driving. I hope this speaker will help clear up some of this confusion. It's my pleasure to introduce Officer Lee Washington from the traffic investigations department."

The audience clapped as Don's brother stepped up to the lectern.

"How often does Eddie call?" Matt whispered to Karen.

"Oh, every now and then."

Lee adjusted the mike as high as it would go. He still had to bend to speak into it.

99

"I'd like to thank Principal Burns for inviting me here today," he said. "We all know it's too late to do anything about Robert Stewart, Randy Chapman, Susan Zorn, and Christopher Walsh, but it's not too late for the rest of you. All I'm going to ask you to do today is listen and think about what I'm going to say. We don't want to lose any more lives."

"You wouldn't really go, would you?" Matt whispered to Karen.

"Shh." Karen held a finger to her lips.

Lee opened a folder. "I'd like to give you a statistic: People between the ages of sixteen and twenty-four represent only one fifth of the licensed drivers in this country. And yet this same group is involved in nearly forty percent of all alcohol-related fatalities. Think about that. One fifth the drivers. Almost half the deaths.

"Bear in mind that not all teenagers killed in drunk-driving accidents are drunk at the time. Many times they haven't been drinking at all, but are simply passengers in cars driven by a teenager who has been drinking. Stop for a moment and think about that. How many of you have ever ridden in a car with someone who had been drinking?"

The kid next to Matt and Karen mumbled, "I do that every time I ride with my old man."

"Here's another statistic," Lee said. "One can of beer, as well as one four-ounce glass of wine, and one one-and-a-half-ounce drink of eighty-six proof liquor are all equally intoxicating. In other words, you get just as drunk on four beers as you do drinking a bottle of wine or four whisky sours."

"That I don't believe," Matt said.

"How many of you just thought to yourself, 'I don't believe that'?" Lee asked.

100

A few hands in the audience went up.

"Come on, be honest."

Karen raised her right hand. With her left she picked up Matt's and made him do the same. A lot more hands went up.

Lee nodded. "It's true. It's been proved over and over in laboratories. It takes very little alcohol to slow your reflexes and cloud your judgment. More than anything else, drunk driving is about bad judgment. It's thinking you've only had a little bit to drink so you must be okay to drive. It's getting into a car with someone else who's been drinking. People do things when they drink that they wouldn't normally do. That's why every time you get into a car you should ask yourself, 'Am I doing the right thing? If I get into this car am I making a mistake?' If the driver has had anything to drink, then the answer is yes.

"Now, most of you know that blood alcohol concentration means the amount of alcohol you have in your blood. Say you have a beer. The beer goes into your stomach and small intestine. From there the alcohol is absorbed directly into your bloodstream. That's why it affects you so quickly. You are legally drunk in this state when your blood alcohol concentration is point one or higher. Tomorrow morning in your homerooms you will each receive a chart that shows how much you have to drink to reach a blood alcohol level of point one and how many drinks you have to consume in an hour to maintain it. Not that I want any of you to try it."

Chuckles rippled through the audience.

"Another thing you should know," Lee continued, "is that you don't have to be legally drunk to drive drunk. Even a blood alcohol concentration of point oh four or oh five can affect your reflexes and judgment. Drinking just two or three beers in one hour can slow your reaction time up to twenty-five percent. It can reduce your visual acuity up to thirty-two percent. It can reduce your recovery time from headlight glare by ten seconds or more, and decrease your peripheral vision as well. It has also been proved that alcohol in your blood reduces your tolerance to injury. In other words, if you are in an accident, you are more likely to be hurt if you've been drinking."

Lee went on for a while longer and then invited the audience to ask questions. Matt was surprised at how many questions kids had. One question, however, stood out from all the others. A kid asked if Lee knew what the blood alcohol concentrations of Chris Walsh and the others were.

"I am forbidden by police department rules to give out that information," Lee said.

Karen nudged Matt. "So the letter couldn't have come from the police department."

"Maybe," Matt replied.

"It's against department rules. You heard him."

Matt nodded. "Yeah, I heard him."

A few more questions and the assembly was over. Matt stood up and started sliding down the aisle past Karen.

"Where are you going?" Karen looked surprised.

"I want to talk to someone," Matt said.

"I thought *we* were going to talk."

"Later. I promise."

He went outside. Lee's patrol car was parked in the visitors' parking area. On the front seat was an empty foam coffee cup and a wrapper from an Egg McMuffin.

A few minutes later, Lee came out of the school. He

smiled when he saw Matt, almost as if he'd expected to find him there.

"How are you?" he asked.

"Okay, Lee." Matt shoved his hands into his pockets. It was colder than he'd thought.

"What's on your mind?"

"What does it mean if a person has a blood alcohol concentration of point one seven?" Matt asked.

"It means he's pretty damn drunk."

"What would the physical effects be?" Matt asked.

"Well, he'd have slurred speech and slowed reflexes. He probably wouldn't be able to walk a straight line."

"Would he be able to drive?"

"That depends on what you mean," Lee said. "If he were still conscious and capable of getting behind the wheel of a car, he could probably make the car go. But I doubt he could see straight enough to steer or keep the car on the road. What usually happens is he goes about ten miles an hour, weaving all over the road, and winds up in a ditch or kissing a tree."

Matt leaned against the car. Was Karen right? Was someone trying to mislead him? If Chris had been that drunk, he never would have made it as far as Flathead Mountain.

"I don't mean to be rude, Matt, but I've got to get back to the station house," Lee said, pulling open the car door. He got in and started the engine. Matt tapped his window and he rolled it down.

"If I have any more questions can I call you?" he asked.

Lee pulled a card out of his pocket and wrote a phone number on the back.

"Call me here," he said, handing Matt the card. "I'm

103

usually in late at night and before eight in the morning. Don't call me at the station. Okay?"

"How come?"

"Just trust me."

"Okay."

Lee winked at him. "Good luck, Matt." He backed the car out and drove away.

Matt headed back inside. He was late for swim practice. As he jogged down the hall toward his locker, he saw Karen waiting for him.

"What are you doing here?" he asked as he pulled his locker open.

"You left in a hurry before," Karen said, ignoring his question.

"Uh, yeah."

"To talk to Lee Washington?"

Matt grinned. "How'd you know?"

"Maybe I just know you, Matt. What did he say?"

"You may be right." He pulled out his athletic bag. "Maybe someone is trying to mislead me."

"So what are you going to do?"

"I'm gonna find out who it is and why they'd do it." Matt slammed his locker closed and started down the hall.

"Uh, Matt?" Karen said.

Matt stopped. "Yeah?"

"I thought we were going to finish talking."

"You'd really go see Eddie Simonds?" Matt asked.

"I might."

"Thompson! You're late!" Schneider was standing with his hands on his hips at the end of the hall.

Matt looked at Karen. "Simonds used to sit in front of me in study hall and pop the zits on the back of his neck."

"I hear he's got a great tan now," Karen replied.

"Shake it, Thompson!" Schneider shouted.

"Call you later," Matt said and started to jog.

"Don't be surprised if the line is busy," Karen called after him.

17

It was dark by the time Matt got home from swim practice. The bus dropped him off at the entrance to Highland Estates and he walked up the street toward his group of town houses. The lights were on in most of the units and Matt could see people eating dinner. It was funny how a lot of families in the development had curtains in their living rooms and bedrooms, but no shades in their kitchens. As if they didn't mind your watching them eat, but you weren't allowed to see anything else.

Ahead, Matt noticed a large dark shadow moving toward him. It was a black pickup truck with its lights off. As the truck passed his group of units, something long and thin poked out the passenger window. He heard three loud hisses followed by clinking sounds.

"Hey!" he shouted.

The truck's headlights flashed on, blinding him. Matt could hear the engine rev and knew the truck was picking up speed, heading right toward him. He dived toward the curb and landed on the grass just as the truck shot past. Matt tried to see who was driving, but the truck was already at the corner, turning onto the street, its tires spinning and screeching on the sand.

He got up and ran across the lawns to Mrs. Walsh's unit. When he got to her door, he banged on it with his fist.

"Mrs. Walsh? Mrs. Walsh!"

For a few moments he heard nothing. Then a frightened voice asked, "Who is it?"

"Matt."

The door opened. Inside, Mrs. Walsh was in her blue robe, clutching Casey to her side. Her eyes were wide and she looked terrified. Casey was whining with fear.

"Are you okay?" Matt asked.

Mrs. Walsh nodded, but she was trembling. "Who were they?"

"I couldn't tell," Matt said, stepping into the house. "They went past me too fast. You sure you're all right?"

"Yes, yes, I think so."

Matt started toward the kitchen.

"What are you doing?" Mrs. Walsh asked.

"Calling the police," Matt said.

Within five minutes two police cars had arrived, along with Matt's mother. The policemen questioned Matt and then spoke to Mrs. Walsh. They stood near the living-room window, looking at three small holes in the glass.

"They're not big enough to have been caused by a gun," one of the cops said.

The other one was crouching on the carpet. A second later he picked up something. The first cop went over and looked at it.

"Pellet," the first cop said.

"From one of those CO_2 guns," said the other.

Mrs. Walsh was sitting on the couch, smoking a cigarette. Matt's mother was sitting next to her. Matt noticed Casey watching from the doorway of the kitchen. Always watching, her eyes wide like one of those nighttime animals in *National Geographic.*

Once they discovered the shots hadn't been from a real gun, the cops seemed impatient to leave. They stood around fidgeting with their hats until Mrs. Walsh noticed, and told them she thought she'd be all right.

The cops put on their hats. "If you see anything that worries you, any cars going slowly past the house, make sure you call us." A moment later they were gone. Mrs. Walsh made a helpless gesture toward Matt's mother.

"Can you do something about that window, Matt?" Mrs. Thompson asked.

"Probably," Matt said. The living-room window was made up of six separate panes of glass. The broken pane was about a foot by a foot and a half. The molding would have to be pried off and a new piece of glass put in. It wasn't something he could do that night.

"You have a piece of cardboard and some tape?" he asked Mrs. Walsh.

"I think so." She got up and went upstairs. Casey followed her, leaving Matt alone in the living room with his mother.

"I think this really scared her," Mrs. Thompson said. "If Casey had been in the room there's a chance she could have been hurt."

"It's pretty sick," Matt said.

"Yes," his mother agreed. "It certainly is."

Mrs. Walsh came back with a shoe box, a pair of scissors, and some masking tape. Matt cut the box to fit over the broken pane and taped it on. Then he measured the window.

"You need a piece of glass twelve by eighteen, and some putty," he told her. "I can probably put it in for you over the weekend."

"I don't know what I'd do without you, Matty," Mrs. Walsh said, her voice quavering. She started to cry. "Oh, God, I'm sorry."

Matt's mother put her arm around her. "You have nothing to be sorry about, Angelica," she said softly, guiding her toward the couch. Over her shoulder she glanced at Matt. He knew what the look meant.

"I'll, uh, see you later," he said, backing toward the door.

His mother didn't come home for another hour. By then Matt had nuked a bunch of hot dogs in the microwave for himself and Peter. Mrs. Thompson came in and surveyed the dirty dishes, the opened hot-dog package on the counter, the extra rolls left out, and the empty thirty-two-ounce bottle of Coke.

"Well, at least you fed yourselves," she said, and started to clean up. Peter went into the den to watch TV, but Matt stayed in the kitchen.

109

"How is she?" he asked.

"Miserable," his mother said. "Miserable and frightened and alone. I swear, if I could get my hands on the kids who threw the garbage on her lawn and shot at her window . . ."

"How do you know they were kids?" Matt asked. "No one saw them."

"You're right, Matt," she said. "But if adults did that . . . it makes me think of terrorists who hijack planes and kill innocent people with bombs. People don't seem to care anymore. About life, about feelings, about what is right and wrong. They have a grudge against something and they think they can do anything they want. Nothing stands in their way."

His mother worked steadily as she talked, cleaning the counter, running the dishwasher, sweeping the floor. Matt watched her. He was thinking about the assembly that afternoon and what Lee had said in the parking lot.

"Something really bothers me about this whole thing," he said.

"You mean the accident?" His mother stopped sweeping for a second. "What is it?"

"It's just a lot of little things right now," Matt said. He told her about the police department's delay in coming up with the cause of the accident, and the questions Lee had asked about the party. Then he told her about the letter with the blood alcohol concentrations, and what Lee had said that afternoon in the parking lot.

"The last thing he said was 'good luck.' Like he knew something. Like he wanted me to keep looking for the answer."

"But you don't know what you're looking for."

Matt shook his head. "Not yet. The way I see it, the

110

only person who could possibly know is Jason, and he won't talk."

Mrs. Thompson leaned on the broom. "Suppose you're right. Suppose something did happen that we don't know about. What would finding out about it change now? Those four kids are dead, Matt. They won't come back."

"It's still not right," Matt said. "If someone's lying we deserve to know. It's too important to shrug off."

His mother started sweeping again. "Intuition tells me it's better left alone, Matt."

"But just a minute ago you said you hated how people thought they could get away with things," Matt said.

Mrs. Thompson nodded. "I know, Matt. But that was in the abstract. It didn't have anything to do with you. This scares me. People who go around shooting out windows scare me. If you're right and it's something the police and mayor know about, then this must be the way they want it. Why go snooping around?"

"Because I want to know. Because Bobby and Chris aren't here to tell their sides of the story."

His mother finished sweeping. She pulled off her apron and hung it in the broom closet. "Matt, it's going to be a long time before I forget how close I came to losing you last week. I know I can't stop you. All I can say is, please, please be careful."

18

The more he thought about it, the more Matt was convinced that Jason was the key. If something was wrong, then he had to know about it. But Jason was out again for two days and when he came back to school he stopped showing up in the cafeteria for lunch. It seemed to Matt that he was avoiding him.

One afternoon after school ended, Matt was in the hall heading toward the locker room for swim practice. Suddenly Marvin Marvick slapped him on the back.

"You hear the news, Matt? Highland High's getting a new pool. It's in the afternoon paper." He held up a folded copy of the *Highland Reporter*. Matt quickly found the story:

STEWARTS TO GIVE HIGH SCHOOL POOL

Highland Hills High School will be getting a new indoor swimming pool from the family of Robert Stewart, Jr., one of the teens killed in a tragic car accident two weeks ago.

The gift was announced this morning by Arthur Crane, president of the school board. Crane called the gesture deeply heartfelt and appreciated. "Anyone who has seen the school's current pool knows how much a new one is needed," he said.

Robert Stewart, Jr., was the captain of the school's swim team.

"It came as a complete surprise to me," the school-board president said. "The phone just rang and it was Mr. Stewart saying he wanted to give the school a pool in his son's memory."

Construction could begin as soon as late spring, Crane said, with the pool possibly in operation in time for next year's swimming season. It will be dedicated to the memory of the Stewart boy, who died when a truck he was riding in along with four others plunged into a mountain ravine. Only one teen survived.

Robert Stewart, Sr., could not be reached for comment this morning. But the Stewart family has a long history of philanthropic goodwill both toward Highland Hills and the state. When told of the gift, Mayor Joseph Torrence said he was not surprised.

"The Stewarts have done tremendous things for this town," he said. "Only most of the time they've done them anonymously."

Samuel Schneider, the coach of the Highland Hills swimming team, said he was "extremely pleased with the news."

"Bobby Stewart was one of the best, if not the best, swimmer Highland High ever had," he said. "He was also a great kid. This pool will be a monument to him so that his memory will remain with us always."

Schneider also said he hoped the gift would lift the spirits of the school, which has been grieving since the four teens met their deaths in a drunk driving accident. A spokesman for Senator William Stewart, the uncle of Robert Stewart, Jr., said that since the death of his nephew, public contributions toward his gubernatorial campaign have doubled. Senator Stewart wants to tighten state controls on teenage alcohol abuse and stiffen penalties for crimes committed under the influence of alcohol and drugs.

Matt finished the story and handed the paper to Marvick. So Bobby's father had actually gone ahead and done it. Most adults couldn't have cared less what teenagers thought. Yet the most successful and influential of them all listened and did care.

Marvin took out a note pad and a pen. "How about a reaction for next month's paper?"

"Well, uh . . ." Matt, caught off guard, fumbled for words. There was no way he could tell Marvin that it had been his idea. No one would believe him. They'd think he was nuts. "I think it's great."

Marvin tapped his pen against the note pad. "That's

it? You don't think you could come up with something a little more insightful?"

"Like what?" Matt asked uneasily.

"I don't know," said Marvin. "But you were Bobby's best friend and now his father is giving the school this pool. What do you think of that?"

Matt felt uncomfortable. "Listen, does this have to be on the record?"

"No." Marvin lowered the note pad.

"Well, this is going to sound a little strange," Matt said. "I mean, I'm really happy and everything, but I also feel a little weird. Like you know how you feel when you get something good and deep inside you don't know why you deserve it?"

Marvin nodded. He put his pen back in his shirt pocket. "Yeah, I know. And you're right, I don't want to print that." He looked up and down the hall as if searching for someone else to interview. "There must be somebody around here who can come up with an inspired quote. If worse comes to worst, I could always make something up and attribute it to a source who asked not to be identified."

"That a boy." Matt patted him on the back and headed for the locker room. He could hear whoops and cheers as he pushed open the doors. Both the JV and varsity swimmers were inside, talking about the news as they changed into their suits.

"Oh, man, this is great!"

"Yeah, good-bye Black Hole."

Matt sat down in front of his locker. Don was sitting a few feet down the bench.

"Some present, huh?" Don said. Matt sensed that he, too, felt uncomfortable about it.

"Yeah, amazing," Matt replied in a low voice.

115

Coach Schneider came in, grinning.

"You see the story, coach?" Shane Stone asked.

"What do you mean, did he see it?" Don asked. "Can't you read, dummy? He's in it."

The swimmers laughed.

"All I can say is," the coach said in a rare jubilant mood, "don't take this lightly. You see this kind of generosity once in a lifetime. It's a very special thing. Now get into your trunks and let's get wet."

Most of the team members had finished changing. By now they all had the black memorial band sewn onto their Speedos. Matt was just closing his locker when Jason came in and sat down on the bench. He spun the dial on his lock.

"Great news, huh?" Matt said, trying once again to be friendly. The bandage on Jason's forehead was gone.

Jason nodded and pulled open his locker. "Too bad we won't be here to use it next year."

"Still, it's nice to know that Bobby will be remembered," Matt said.

Without answering, Jason started unbuttoning his shirt. He was staring into his locker. Matt looked around and realized they were the only two left in the locker room.

"Say, Jason, did you ever talk to Lee Washington?" he asked.

Jason gave him a sideways glance. "Yeah, a couple of times."

"Did you ever get the feeling from him," Matt started to ask, "that something wasn't quite—"

Jason shook his head. "No."

That's funny, Matt thought, I didn't even have a chance to finish the sentence.

"Didn't it seem like it took a long time for the police

116

to come up with the cause?" Matt asked. "Especially when it seemed so obvious."

"Don't ask me," Jason said, pulling off his pants. "I'm not a cop."

"I heard there was some kind of problem," Matt said. "The mayor was involved."

"Then go talk to him," Jason said curtly.

Matt studied him. "Mind if I ask what's bugging you? Ever since the accident you've been acting weird."

Jason turned and glared at him. "You really want to know what's bugging me? It's this totally phony act you're putting on, Thompson. Like we're friends or something. It's a lot of crap and you know it. The only reason you were ever friendly to me was because of Bobby. You never really wanted me around, so you can cut the BS."

"Okay, fine," Matt said. "But I still want to know what happened in Chris's truck that night."

"Nothing happened."

"Was someone else there?"

Jason pulled on his bathing suit. "No."

"Was there another car?"

"No."

"Was something going on with you and Bobby and the girls?"

Jason laughed and got up. "You got a great imagination, Thompson." He headed toward the pool.

Matt felt his frustration growing. He put his arm against the wall, blocking Jason's path. "I'm serious."

"Buzz off."

Jason tried to push his arm out of the way. Matt shoved him against the wall and held him there with his left hand. His right hand was drawn back in a fist, itching to smash him in the face.

117

Jason looked scared for a second, but then he sneered. "Go ahead, Thompson. What are you going to prove? That Bobby liked you more? You think it's gonna go down in the record books that you were his best friend? Nobody cares, you jerk."

Matt let go. "It's not that."

Jason smirked. "Sure, Thompson, sure." He walked past him and went out to the pool.

At dinner, Peter was wearing his Walkman again.

"Off," Mrs. Thompson ordered.

Peter sighed dramatically and turned off the tape.

"Off." Mrs. Thompson pointed at the earphones still on his head.

"Why can't I leave them on?" he whined.

"What's the point if the music's off?" Matt asked.

"I can pretend," Peter said.

"Pretend?" Matt scowled.

"Not at the dinner table," Mrs. Thompson said firmly.

Peter made a big show of removing the headphones and letting them rest around his neck. "Just wait till I get my drums."

Matt smiled.

"What's so funny?" Peter asked.

"Since when are you getting drums?" Matt asked back.

"Grandpa said if I pulled my average up to a B he'd buy me a set," Peter said.

"When did he say that?" asked Matt.

"Christmas, barf brain."

"Grandpa can't even remember yesterday. You really think he's gonna remember a promise he made over a month ago?"

"You'll see, toilet face."

"Peter, take your dinner to your room," Mrs. Thompson snapped.

"Wha . . . Great! It would be a pleasure not to have to eat with you dorks." Peter jumped up and took his plate. A second later he was gone.

Mrs. Thompson sighed and returned to her meal. "I assume you saw the paper today."

"Couldn't miss it," Matt answered.

"Talk about bittersweet victories."

"Yeah, I know."

"Still, it must be a sincere gesture," Mrs. Thompson said. "I just hope it doesn't hurt Senator Stewart's chances."

"What do you mean?" Matt asked.

"Hughes is so desperate that he'll do anything to discredit his opponents," his mother explained. "That includes accusing the Stewarts of trying to buy sympathy votes. Of course, when you think of the size of this town, it doesn't make sense to spend millions on a pool just for a few thousand votes. Not to mention the fact that this is Stewart country to begin with."

"Everything comes down to politics," Matt said.

"Politics *and* money," said his mother. "Especially in an election year. Giving the school a new pool is a lovely idea. I just wish the timing had been better."

Matt nodded. He was dying to tell her the idea had been his. But he knew she'd tell her friends and before long the town would think he was bragging. Besides, ideas were cheap. It was the Stewarts who were coming up with the money.

19

On Saturdays Karen waitressed at Olga's House of Pancakes until three P.M. Matt waited in the parking lot until she came out.

"Well, look who's here," she said caustically.

"I have to talk to you," Matt said.

"About us or about the accident? Because if it's about the accident you might as well save your breath."

"Huh?"

"Because that's all you ever want to talk about,"

Karen said. "You never called me the night you said you would. Someone slips a letter under your door and you think you have to become Thomas Magnum."

"This is important, Karen."

"To who?"

"To me, and it should be to you too."

"Give me a break, Matt." She started to open the door to her car. Matt stopped the door with his hand.

"Karen, I'm sorry," he said. "I really am. I'm sorry about what I said that night at dinner and I'm sorry that I didn't call. But I'm not sorry about what I'm doing. I really think something's wrong and I'm going to find out what it is. And I—I just wish you wouldn't go to see that dirt bag Simonds."

Her face softened. "You mean that?"

"Totally."

"And you came here to tell me that?"

"Well . . . yes."

She put her arms around his neck and kissed him. Matt inhaled the aroma of perfume mixed with maple syrup.

"So, uh, were you planning to do anything this afternoon?" he asked after she let go.

"Nothing important. Why?"

"Feel like taking a ride?"

"Sure. Where?"

"How about up to the mountains?"

"Okay, great. Let's go back to my house so I can change."

"You can go just the way you are," Matt said.

Karen scowled. "In my uniform?"

"Sure. We're just going for a ride."

She let him drive. The weather had finally cleared and the sun was shining. They took the highway west toward the mountains, passing the suburbs and rising through the white foothills. It was a steady climb uphill and the glare of the late afternoon sun off the new snow was so bright he had to put on sunglasses. The mountains were sheathed in white, the jagged peaks spearing little puffs of clouds.

Thirty minutes later and three thousand feet higher, Matt turned off the highway. At the bottom of the exit ramp was an Arco station. The snow at that altitude was much deeper than down below. Around the station it had been plowed into ten-foot banks to clear a path for cars. Matt passed the station and turned onto Route 9, a narrow two-lane highway. He followed it for about ten minutes and then made a left onto Flathead Mountain Road.

The road was a switchback that zigzagged up the side of the mountain. The grade was steep and barely wide enough for two cars. On both sides plowed snow rose above the car's windows.

According to the newspaper stories, the accident had occurred two hundred yards north of the turnoff from Route 9. Matt drove up to the spot. It was right at the switchback—traffic going up the mountain had to make a sharp left turn and head back in the other direction.

At the end of the switchback a temporary wooden barrier with a big red arrow directed drivers to turn. Matt parked the car on the side of the road.

"Why are we stopping here?" Karen asked.

"I want to see something," Matt said. "It'll just take a second."

He got out. The air was cold, crisp, and dry. He pulled on his jacket. The sun had gone behind the mountain, throwing an icy shadow on the few inches of fresh snow that had fallen during the night.

THE ACCIDENT

As Matt got closer to the wooden barrier his insides began to twist and churn. With the exception of the funerals, nothing about the events of the last two weeks had seemed real to him. The accident still could have been a bunch of made-up stories for all he knew. Bobby, Chris, and the others could have taken off for Mexico for a couple of weeks. The coffins could have contained dummies. But as Matt walked toward the wooden barrier, he knew that on the other side was one more chunk of the truth.

He reached the barrier and looked around. On the other side was a gaping hole in the wall of plowed snow. Matt could see what was left of the guardrail. The heavy metal cables hung down over the edge of the mountain. The metal post that normally held the cables had been completely uprooted. The Blazer must have really been flying, he thought.

Feeling a little dizzy, he walked around the barrier. Beyond the guardrail the mountain fell away in a steep slope. About thirty feet below were broken tree trunks and trees with raw gashes in the bark. Beyond that was nothing but air—a straight drop into the ravine. It was a long way down. The rescuers weren't kidding when they said it was a miracle Jason had survived. There were only a couple of trees he could have landed in. Otherwise he would have fallen straight down the rocky cliff.

"I should push you," Karen said. Matt turned and saw that she was standing behind him. He hadn't heard her get out of the car. She was looking down into the ravine and he could tell she wasn't really mad.

"I'm sorry," Matt said. "I just had to come out here."

"Why did you have to bring me?" she asked.

"I don't know. I just wanted you to come."

He slipped his arm around her waist and they stood for a while, looking down into the ravine. The breeze blew a fine dust of snow off the trees and into their faces. A hawk circled in the air above.

"What did you expect?" Karen asked.

"I don't know."

"Maybe you just needed final proof," she said softly.

Matt nodded. He felt Karen pull his arm.

"Come on, let's go."

They got back into the car and drove down the mountain. Matt felt lightheaded again, imagining what it must have been like inside the Blazer that split second before impact. Sheer, unimaginable terror. He was almost past the Arco station when he saw something and hit the brakes.

"What?" Karen asked.

Matt pointed at a wreck pressed up against a snowbank. It was hard to believe it was the same truck he'd seen in Chris's driveway two weeks before. He made a sharp turn into the station and stopped next to the gas pump.

"Want to come?" Matt said, getting out.

Karen shook her head. A man wearing green coveralls and a dirty orange vest came out of the office.

"Fill 'er up?" the man asked.

Matt nodded, hoping he had enough money. "Regular unleaded."

The man started to fill the tank. Matt pretended to stretch and then strolled toward the Blazer as if he were just getting some fresh air.

The roof was crushed in. The sides looked as if some giant had gone at it with a super-huge sledgehammer. The hood and passenger door were missing and all the windows were smashed. Inside, the seats were ripped from their mounts. Matt began to feel queasy again. He couldn't stop thinking about what it must have been like being inside, falling . . . He turned and walked away, taking deep breaths. The man was watching him.

"What happened to that?" Matt asked innocently.

"Went off the side of the mountain," the man said. "You musta heard about it. Four kids killed, includin' Senator Stewart's nephew."

Matt shook his head. "Must've missed it."

"Oh? You not from around here?" the man asked.

"Coopersville," Matt said.

The man tugged at his earlobe. "Boy, I thought everyone in the state would've heard about this one."

"Four kids, huh?" Matt said.

"Yep," the man said. "The amazin' thing is there was a fifth who actually lived. Got thrown out near the top and landed in a tree. Just had a few scratches."

"Doesn't seem possible," Matt said.

"Sure don't."

"I mean, how could he possibly . . . ?" Matt purposely left the question open ended.

"Guess it depends on where you're sittin'," said the man. He put the gas cap on the tank. Matt gave him some money, and the man started counting out change.

"Just out of curiosity," Matt said. "Where *was* he sitting?"

"Who?" the man asked, concentrating on the change.

"That kid, the one who survived."

The man looked at Matt and then down at Karen's car. His face hardened. He handed Matt a couple of bills and some silver. Then he shoved his hands into the pockets of his coveralls.

"Next time you tell someone you're from Coopersville," he said, "better take that Highlands High

125

bumper sticker off your car first." He turned and walked away.

"Now do you believe me?" Matt asked. They were almost at Karen's house. She had been quiet for most of the trip back from the mountains.

"Believe you about what?" she asked absently.

"That something's going on. I mean, you saw how that guy at the Arco station shut up once he realized I was from Highland Hills."

"Maybe he just noticed that you'd lied," said Karen. "You're not very good at it, you know."

"What's that supposed to mean?"

"You lied to me," Karen said. "You said you wanted to take me for a ride in the mountains when all you really wanted to do was use my car."

"That's not true. I could've taken my mother's car."

"Why didn't you?"

"I already told you," Matt said. "I wanted you to come. I want you to believe me." He turned onto her street.

"The only thing I believe is that you're fixated on this accident," Karen said.

Matt pulled into her driveway and stopped. He looked across at her. "Okay, try telling me what taking you out for pizza and a movie tonight has to do with the accident."

Karen smiled. "Nothing. And let's keep it that way."

"I thought you weren't going to think about it," Karen said. They were sitting in the Pizza Hut at the Highland Hills Mall.

"I'm not," Matt told her.

Karen rolled her eyes. "Matt, do you realize you

haven't said a word to me in the last five minutes? Have you even heard a word of what I've been talking about?"

"Uh . . ." Matt searched his memory. But his mind had been off in hyperspace. He shrugged.

Karen dabbed her lips with her napkin and started to get up. "Every time you do this to me, I swear to myself that it's the last time. But this time I'm serious, it really is."

"Wait," Matt said quickly. "You're right and I'm sorry. Just let me make one phone call and then I swear to God I won't think about it again for the rest of the night."

"You swear?"

"Cross my heart and hope to die."

Karen sighed. "Go ahead."

Matt got up and went to the pay phone near the rest rooms. He took out Lee Washington's card and dialed the number.

Lee sounded sleepy.

"I didn't wake you, did I?" Matt asked.

"Nope, I was just settling down with a bowl of popcorn to watch an old movie. So what's up?"

"I know something's going on," Matt said.

Lee was silent. Matt could hear the faint sound of a television in the background.

"I have a feeling you know what it is," Matt said.

"Department policy strictly forbids me from discussing the investigation, Matt."

"Yeah, right," Matt said, pressing on. "But you gave me your home number. I've been wondering about that. You wouldn't have done it if everything was the way the police said it was. That's why you don't want me to call you at the station."

Silence.

"Isn't it your duty to make sure people know the truth?" Matt asked.

"It's my duty to investigate traffic fatalities," Lee said.

"But if someone is lying, doesn't it bother you?"

All Matt heard was a Pepsi commercial.

"I have a feeling you don't like what's going on any more than I do," Matt went on. "But you can't do anything about it because you'd be breaking the rules and then they could nail you. You didn't spend four years on foot patrol to blow it now."

Lee cleared his throat.

"It's not fair," Matt said. "Four friends of mine are dead and no one will tell me what happened."

"People try to do what they think is right," Lee said.

"What does that mean?"

"Just what I said."

Matt sighed. He wasn't getting anywhere. But Lee was his last chance and there had to be a way to get him to talk.

"Okay, listen," Matt told him. "I think you know what's going on. You say you can't tell me, but I get the feeling you want me to find out. Otherwise you wouldn't even be on the phone with me right now. All I want to know is, should I keep going or not?"

All he heard was another commercial.

"Come on, damn it, tell me," Matt said forcefully.

"I can't stop you," Lee said.

"You can't stop me," Matt repeated. "I think that means you want me to keep going."

Lee cleared his throat again. Was that his way of saying yes?

"Who should I talk to?" Matt asked, excited.

"I, uh, have to go, Matt."

"Does Jason know? Or Principal Burns?"

"I'm sorry, Matt."

Matt stared at the pay phone dial. Lee couldn't talk without risking his job. But then, maybe he'd already said enough. "Okay, Lee. Thanks."

"Anytime, Matt."

Matt hung up. He was certain now. Something was going on. All he had to do was plot his next move and figure out the right questions to ask. He felt so good he practically skipped back into the restaurant.

Karen was gone.

For one crazy moment he thought she'd been kidnapped by the same people who were trying to cover up the accident. Then he noticed the napkin on his plate. It was half soaked with pizza grease, but when he picked it up, he could make out the message: *Dear Matt, I didn't believe you.*

20

He tried calling her a couple of times that night and the next morning, but he kept getting her answering machine. Matt suspected she was there, sitting on her bed, listening to his messages.

Later he went over to the Walshes' to fix the broken window. Mrs. Walsh was wearing a dark dress. Matt knew she'd gone to church that morning. Before Chris died she'd never been a churchgoer.

"Matty, I have to go out and do some food shopping,"

she said. "We're down to practically nothing. Do you mind if I leave Casey here with you?"

"No problem," Matt said. He took his tools into the living room. The house was dirty and gloomy. The ashtray on the living-room table was full of butts and gum wrappers. A pile of old newspapers and magazines lay on the floor near the couch.

He could hear Mrs. Walsh in the kitchen, talking to Casey. "Don't make a pest of yourself."

A moment later she came out. "If you finish before I get back, don't worry, you can leave Casey by herself."

"Okay."

Mrs. Walsh left and Matt got to work. He found the new pane of glass wrapped in brown paper and held it up to the window to make sure it fit. Then he took a screwdriver and a hammer out of his toolbox and started to pry off the molding around the broken pane.

He heard a scratching sound and turned around. Casey had climbed onto the couch. She was wearing a yellow dress with pleats, white stockings, and black patent leather shoes. Church clothes. When he looked at her, she ducked and hid her face behind a pillow. Matt chuckled and went back to work. Strange little kid.

Casey crept closer. She squatted on the carpet a few feet away, cocked her head, and eyed him. Like a pigeon.

"Look," Matt said. "You want to see how to fix a window? You should learn so you can do it next year when I'm at college."

Casey didn't answer. She just stayed there, squatting on the carpet, watching.

Matt pressed the screwdriver against the molding and tapped it gently with the hammer. "See? The molding is what holds the glass in. So you have to take it

131

out like this. But you have to be careful you don't break the glass."

Matt pried the molding off. Casey came a little closer. She seemed more interested in his toolbox than the window. Matt took out a ratchet. He turned it in his hand and it made a clicking sound. Casey smiled. Matt gave it to her.

"It's called a ratchet," he said.

Casey turned the wrench in her hand, making it click rapidly.

"Hah . . . hit."

Matt stopped working and turned around. Casey had actually talked! It was the first time he'd ever heard her say something.

"That was close," he said. "But it's ratchet. Rat . . . chet."

Casey tried again. "Hat . . . chet." She couldn't make *r* sounds. Still, it was a pretty good attempt.

Matt held up the screwdriver. "Screwdriver."

"Scu . . . divuh."

He held up the hammer. "Hammer."

"Hammuh," Casey said.

"Yeah, that's right." Matt grinned at her.

She grinned back.

Matt kept talking to her as he took out the broken glass and put in the new pane. Casey repeated the words he said. But then she started to play a game. He said "window" and she said "gwass."

"No," Matt corrected her. "Window."

Casey shook her head. "Gwass."

"Oh, I get it," Matt said. "Glass. Windows are made of glass."

Casey nodded.

Matt held up the tube of putty. "Putty."

132

"Siwwy," Casey said.

"Yeah, silly," said Matt. "Silly Putty."

Then Casey pointed out the window. A couple of guys were walking down the street wearing denim jackets and smoking cigarettes. As they passed, she said, "Kwiss."

Matt looked at her, not certain what to say. "But Chris's gone."

"Kwiss in Hewwen. Took his tuck."

"Will you ever see Chris again?" Matt asked carefully.

Casey nodded eagerly. "In Hewwen."

Matt felt a pang. She probably thought Heaven was a place you could visit on weekends. She probably couldn't wait until her mother took her to see him.

"Do you, uh, think you'll see him soon?" Matt asked.

Casey looked down and picked a string off her dress. Her forehead furrowed. She'd probably been wondering the same thing.

Matt finished puttying the new window. He'd always thought Casey was retarded. But she wasn't. She might have had trouble talking and learning, but she understood things. She could think. No wonder she watched everyone. She was probably trying to figure out why she didn't fit in.

Matt wrapped the old piece of glass in newspaper and put it in the garbage. He spent a few minutes picking up paint chips and splinters from the living-room carpet. When he was finished, he put the tools in the box.

"I'm gonna go now," he told her.

Casey followed him to the front door. The kid was alone all the time. Now, without Chris, she'd be even more alone.

"Hey, if you ever want to come over to my house," Matt said, "just come over, okay?"

Casey scowled at him and stared at the ground. Matt had the feeling she understood him. But going over to his house was something she'd never do.

21

- -

At lunch on Monday Matt headed for the swimmers' table in the cafeteria. Don and Shane and some of the other guys were already sitting there. As soon as Don saw him coming he got up and gestured for Matt to follow him. They walked through the cafeteria and into the hall outside. The only other people in sight were two girls, late for lunch, coming down the hall toward them.

"What's going on?" Matt asked.

"Just wait," Don said in a low voice, letting the two girls go into the cafeteria.

"What was that all about?" Matt asked, mystified. They were alone now.

"Don't bother my brother anymore," Don said.

"What? Why?"

"Just don't, okay? Forget the accident, forget everything. And don't ask me any questions at the table in front of the other guys."

"I wasn't going to ask you anything," Matt protested. "I was just going to sit down and eat lunch."

Don gave him a skeptical look.

"Okay, maybe I would have asked something, but so what?" Matt said.

"Why can't you leave it alone?" Don asked harshly. "You're not gonna bring anyone back."

Matt stared at him. "Wait a minute. Who said I can't talk to Lee? Did he tell you to say that?"

Don shrugged. "Just drop it. What's done is done."

"No way," Matt said. "Something's going on. That's why no one will talk to me. That's why you're telling me to forget about it. Something happened that no one wants us to know about."

The cafeteria doors opened and three guys came out and went down the hall. Don waited until they were out of earshot.

"You think you have to know about everything that goes down around here?" he asked. "Half this town's got deeds on their houses that say they can't sell to blacks. I don't see you getting too upset about that. And what about every time it snows? Guess what's the last part of town to get plowed? The black part. And if a garbage truck breaks down, you know whose garbage don't get picked up? You going to do anything about that?"

"What are you talking about?"

"A lot of crap against black people goes down in this town and I don't see whites doing anything about it," Don said. "So why should my brother do anything for you?"

Matt stared at him. This wasn't Don talking. It was Don pretending to be someone else.

"Somebody got to you," Matt told him. "The same way they got to Jason. Was it Lee? Tell me who it was. Tell me what's going on."

"What's going on is you're crazy, man," said Don. "No one got to me. What do you think this is, the movies? You think they're gonna blow up my grandmother if I talk to you? I got my own problems, Matt. And so does Lee. And we don't need you nosing around asking questions."

Don turned to go back into the cafeteria, but Matt grabbed his arm. "Everything you just said was pure bull and you know it. It's like a speech you've been rehearsing all day. I don't know what's going on and I don't want to get you or your brother in trouble. I just want to know who got to you."

"You're crazy, man." Don tried to shake Matt's hand off, but Matt held tight.

"I'm not."

Don looked up and down the hall, refusing to look at him.

"For Bobby's sake," Matt said urgently. "I won't tell anyone you told me. I promise."

Don looked at him.

"Come on, Don."

"Swear to God you won't tell?"

"Absolutely. On my mother's grave."

Don sighed. "Okay, listen. No one got to me and Lee doesn't know anything about this, but I know you've been bugging him. You got to understand something, Matt. My brother's only the second black cop ever hired in this town, and the first one quit after two weeks. The only reason they hired Lee was to meet government quotas on minorities so they could qualify for federal funds. You know he was on foot patrol for four years. Out on the street freezing his butt off all winter and sweating all summer while the white cops snoozed in their patrol cars. They used to drive by and laugh at him, Matt. *Cops in the same department.* But he wanted to prove something, so he hung in."

"I hear you," Matt said.

"So finally they had to promote him," Don said. "Like he had four years' seniority and a perfect record and if they tried to promote white rookies over him he could've sued. So they put him in charge of accident investigations and stuck him in a closet. Some promotion."

"Yeah, but—"

"Wait." Don cut him off. "Get this, Matt. Last Friday the chief of police calls him into his office and asks him if he's had any problems with the investigation on Chris's accident. My brother's no fool, so he says no, everything's fine. So the chief goes, 'That's good, let's keep it that way. And by the way, you're being promoted to detective.' "

Matt felt a tingling sensation in his ears.

Don smiled. "That's right. All of a sudden my brother's got a gold badge and a new unmarked car and he's the first black detective ever in Highland Hills. That make it any clearer to you?"

138

Matt looked down at the floor. "Yeah. That helps. Thanks for telling me."

Don shoved his hands in his pockets. "Don't sweat it, dude. Just remember your promise."

For the rest of the day, Matt's mind was on the accident and nothing else. Whoever was behind this mystery had long arms. They reached all the way up to the Arco station on Flathead Mountain and deep into the Highland Hills police department. They even reached to Highland Hills High.

That afternoon the Black Hole seemed extra cold. Matt and the other swimmers did laps and practiced relays. It seemed as if Coach Schneider took pity on them for once, because he ended the practice early.

Back in the locker room, Matt sat with the other swimmers on the bench, doing the combination on his lock. He was still wearing his wet Speedo and had a damp towel draped over his shoulders. He was shivering. Next to him Don was so cold his teeth were chattering.

Matt had just opened his locker when Schneider shouted, "Thompson, in my office."

"Can I change first, coach?"

"No."

Matt stood up. Don and the other swimmers glanced at him, but he couldn't read their expressions. He walked down the cold concrete floor barefoot and went into the coach's office, keeping the towel over his shoulders. The office was ice cold in spite of a small electric heater on the floor aimed toward the desk where Schneider was sitting.

Matt closed the door and sat down on a wooden chair. The floor felt like ice under his feet. Goose bumps ran

up and down his arms. Schneider leaned back and put
his hands behind his massive head. In back of him was a
shelf full of dusty trophies—almost all of them were for
track, the other sport he coached.

"I hear that you've been asking questions about the
accident," the coach said.

Surprised by this, Matt almost asked how he knew,
but he caught himself.

"Something bothering you about it?" the coach
asked.

"Maybe."

Schneider leaned forward ominously, placing his
elbows on the desk. His forearms were as thick as Matt's
thighs. "Let me ask you a question, Thompson. Do you
have any idea how unbelievable it is that the Stewarts
want to build us an Olympic-size indoor pool? In a
hundred years I'd never dream that someone would
just go and build us a new pool."

Before Matt could answer, the coach leaned closer.
"Now listen to me, Thompson. I don't know what your
beef is, but I do know that if you keep asking nosy
questions you may screw us right out of that pool.
Maybe you don't care because you're graduating this
year and that pool won't be completed until next fall.
But I care. And the rest of the team cares. And all the
swimmers who follow in the years to come are going to
care that some wiseass with an ax to grind screwed us
out of the one damn thing we needed to make a winning team."

"So you're gonna cut me," Matt said, chagrined.

Schneider looked surprised. "Oh, no, Thompson, I
wouldn't dream of cutting you. I want to keep you on
the team. I want you around the other swimmers so
that they can appreciate what you're doing."

The coach sat back in his chair. "There is one other thing. Colleges consider your admission conditional until you complete your senior year of high school. Think about that, Thompson. A lot could happen between now and June that might make them change their minds."

Matt couldn't help smiling. Someone, somewhere, was trying very hard to keep a lid on the truth.

Schneider frowned. "You think it's funny?"

Matt shook his head.

"I don't know, Thompson, I don't think I got the message across to you," the coach said. "You better get yourself back out to the pool. Your butterfly's been looking pretty weak lately. Give me twenty laps."

"But I don't swim butterfly," Matt argued. "And practice is over."

"Not for you it isn't."

Matt gulped for a breath. He'd never done more than fifty yards of butterfly in his life. It was the most tiring stroke in swimming and he was sure he'd drown before he'd finish twenty laps. Even after the other swimmers had showered and left, he was still in the pool, sputtering, struggling to lift both arms together above the water.

Just eight more laps. His lips were blue, his eyes burned from chlorine, his fingers were numb and wrinkled like prunes. If he could just sneak in a couple of breast strokes . . .

"Butterfly, Thompson!" Schneider shouted from the bleachers.

Matt caught a mouthful of water and nearly choked. His shoulders were killing him. He reached the wall and turned, thankful for once that the pool was so small.

141

Seven . . . six . . . five laps to go. Now he had to stop and rest between each stroke, sticking his head out of the water like a turtle and gasping.

"Swim, Thompson!" Schneider yelled.

Matt struggled to kick and swim. Finally, with two laps to go, he couldn't get his arms above the surface.

"I said swim, you wussy!"

Matt rolled onto his back, too exhausted to swim another stroke. All because Schneider thought he didn't want the new pool. He wanted to scream, *"It was my idea in the first place, you dummy!"* But the hell with it. No one would believe him now. So he'd just stay in the middle of the pool all night. If Schneider wanted him, he could come in and get him.

"Swim, wussy!"

Matt shook his head. His vision was blurred. The lights had fuzzy halos. He listened to the water lapping the sides of the pool.

Schneider hopped down from the bleachers. "I always knew you had no guts, Thompson." He walked over to the edge of the pool.

Matt stood in the water, breathing hard and watching him.

"Get out. I can't leave with you in the pool. You might drown."

Matt didn't move.

"I said, get out!"

Matt swam slowly to the side. He reached for the edge and tried to pull himself up and out, but he was too tired, his arms and shoulders too sore. He tried again, got halfway out, then slid back into the water.

With a disgusted look on his face, Schneider stepped toward Matt and offered his hand. Matt reached up and Schneider grabbed him by the wrist and yanked hard.

142

A bolt of pain shot through Matt's shoulder, as if his arm were being pulled out of the socket, but he couldn't twist out of the coach's grip. Schneider dragged Matt out of the pool, making sure he smashed his elbows and knees against the pool's edge. Then the coach pulled him a few feet across the rough concrete floor. The skin on Matt's knees and ankles tore on the cold, wet concrete. Before he could get his footing, Schneider let go. Matt fell on his side, gasping for breath and too exhausted to move. His knees and ankles stung. His shoulder throbbed.

"Wussy." Schneider turned and stalked away.

Minutes passed. Matt lay on the cold, wet concrete and didn't move. When he finally felt the energy to get to his feet, he saw that one of his elbows and both of his knees and ankles were bleeding. His arms, legs, and chest muscles were so sore they burned, and he couldn't lift his right arm higher than his shoulder. He heard a door slam and knew that Schneider had gone home.

He limped into the locker room, dabbed the blood off his knees and ankles with his towel, and pulled on his socks and pants. He got his shirt on, but he couldn't get his right arm high enough to pull on his sweater. Instead he draped it over his shoulders. By the time he'd finished dressing he'd missed the last bus. He left the locker room and stepped out into the empty, dark hallway. The only lights were at the end of the corridor. He limped toward the phone booth at the main entrance and called Karen.

It wasn't hard to persuade her to come get him. He told her he was hurt and didn't want his mother to know. She said she'd be right there.

He waited alone in the school vestibule, looking out

at the dark. Two cars were left in the parking lot and only a few lights were still on in the building. Except for the janitors, he was probably the last person left on school property. And the last person left in the world who wanted to know what had really happened the night of the accident. Maybe he was being stupid. He'd been searching for an answer for nearly two weeks, and he still didn't have a clue. Maybe Don was right. You didn't have to uncover every truth, expose all lies to the air. Bobby, Chris, Randy, and Susie weren't coming back.

Headlights turned into the school entrance. He pulled open the door and limped to the curb.

"Are you okay?" Karen asked anxiously, pushing open the car door.

"Sort of." Matt groaned as he eased himself into the car. He'd asked Karen to bring him aspirin and something to wash it down with. She gave him the tablets and a can of warm V-8 juice. Matt winced.

"I grabbed the first thing I saw," she said.

Matt swallowed the pills and juice. It wasn't as bad as he'd expected. He straightened his legs under the dashboard and grimaced.

"Did he really work you over?" Karen asked.

"Not in a way that he could get into trouble for," Matt said. "He just made me swim a ton of extra laps and then yanked me out of the pool when I was too tired to get out myself."

"Why?"

"He thinks I'm gonna do something that'll make the Stewarts take back the pool."

Karen pulled away from the school.

"Where do you want to go?" she asked.

"I don't know. Can we just drive for a while?"

"I guess." She always leaned forward when she drove, her chin just a couple of inches from the steering wheel, as if she thought the closer she was to the windshield, the better she could see. It made Matt nervous, but traffic was light.

"Listen," Matt said. "I want to tell you something, but you have to swear you won't tell anyone. Not your best friend, not your parents, not anyone."

"Okay."

"That new pool was my idea. After Chris's funeral I went to the Stewarts' house. Mr. Stewart said he wanted to do something in Bobby's memory and I suggested the pool."

"So?"

"Don't you see? It was my idea, but someone's trying to turn it all around and make me the villain. I mean, it's crazy."

Karen glanced at him. "Matt, I want to say something, but I don't want you to take it the wrong way."

"What?"

"I think maybe you should talk to someone."

"Who?"

"A psychologist."

Matt stared at her. "You don't believe that it was my idea?"

"Of course I believe you," she said. "But I also think you're having a hard time accepting what's happened and it might help to talk to a professional."

"You think this mystery I'm trying to solve is just something I made up so I wouldn't have to face the fact that Bobby and the others are dead?"

"Is it?" Karen asked.

Matt shook his head wearily. "I don't believe this."

"Matt, you have no evidence that anything is wrong."

145

"I know it took the police six days to announce the cause of the accident when it should have taken ten minutes," Matt said. "I know someone sent me the blood alcohol concentrations and that's information no one is supposed to have. I know Lee Washington said something funny was going on and all of a sudden he's been promoted to detective. I know Jason won't talk about it and that guy at the Arco station shut up as soon as he figured out what I was getting at."

"But you still have no idea what *it* is," said Karen. "You don't even know if those things have any relationship to each other. They could all be separate, unrelated occurrences. For instance, you don't really know why Don's brother got a promotion, or where those blood alcohol figures came from. Or if they're even real. And you certainly don't know why it took the police so long to announce the cause. *You've* decided they're all related. But there's no reason for anyone else to think they are."

With his fingertip, Matt wrote *Wrong* backwards on the foggy windshield. The one person in the world he needed to believe and support him . . . *"You're not that good a skier."* . . . Maybe she'd been right last time, but this time she was wrong.

A few minutes later, Karen steered the car into Highland Estates. As they pulled into Matt's driveway, he noticed a red-and-white FOR SALE sign on the Walshes' front lawn.

Karen turned off the engine. "Are you surprised?"

"Shouldn't I be?" Matt asked bitterly. "They're chasing her out of town."

"God, Matt, don't you think you're being a little dramatic?"

Matt glared at her. "No, I don't. She didn't do any-

146

thing and she's being persecuted. Four of our friends are dead and you act like you don't even care."

Karen's jaw dropped. "Are you serious? You think I don't care? If I didn't care I would have told you to go to hell two weeks ago. Do you have any idea what you've been like? Nobody else in the world exists except you, Bobby, and Chris. The only thing you've wanted me for is transportation. All I'm supposed to say is 'You're right' and 'Attention, your door is open.'"

"You're so full of it," Matt almost shouted.

"I'm full of it?" Karen yelled. "You've created this whole mystery just to avoid dealing with the truth, and I'm the one who's full of it?"

"And what do *you* think the truth is?" Matt snapped back.

"I think the truth is that you don't want to deal with what's really happened. Your friends are dead and you can't face it so you spend all your time in this stupid fantasy."

"That is a complete and total load of crap," Matt said slowly.

"Get out," Karen said.

"At least I care."

"I said, get out!"

"With pleasure." Matt got out and slammed the door.

22

The next day Matt quit the swimming team. He would have preferred smashing Schneider in the face with a baseball bat, but reason prevailed. The next best thing just might be proving he was right about the accident, that whatever had happened the night Bobby and the others died, it wasn't what the police and newspapers claimed.

As Mrs. Thompson had predicted, Governor Hughes attacked the Stewarts on the pool issue. He accused them of currying voter sympathy and announced the formation of a special state panel to investigate voter registration patterns.

"Harassment," Marvin Marvick said at lunch. He and Matt were sitting at a table near the Coke machine. Marvin was tilted back in his chair with his feet up on the table, the *Highland Reporter* spread out in his lap. Matt kept looking over at the swimmers' table, halfway across the cafeteria, where Jason and Don and some of the others were eating and talking.

"As soon as your average unregistered Joe Schmo hears that there's a special panel investigating voter registration, there's no way he's going to register," Marvin was saying. "Hughes may be slime, but he's not stupid. He knows that the majority of people registering after the swimming pool announcement are going to be Stewart supporters. So he's trying to scare them off."

Matt half listened. At the swimmers' table everyone became quiet while Jason said something. The weird thing was that Matt had always assumed that Jason had joined the team just to hang around with Bobby. But Jason was still on the team, still going to practice every afternoon in the icy Black Hole. The guys around Jason broke out in laughter. Matt looked down at his sandwich and wondered what had happened to his appetite.

It was three days before he could get his right arm higher than his shoulder. After school he'd watch real estate agents bring prospective buyers to the Walsh unit. He couldn't blame Mrs. Walsh for wanting to move away, but it made him angry anyway.

Friday evening after dinner he sat in the den with his

mother and watched the news on TV. They were reporting on the gubernatorial campaign.

"The race is really starting to heat up," his mother said as they listened to a reporter talk about Senator Stewart's "tough new proposals concerning drivers under the influence of alcohol or drugs."

The story cut to a news clip of the senator addressing a meeting of Jaycees. He was standing on the dais, flanked on both sides by fat, bald men eating dessert. He looked polished and unruffled in his coal-gray pinstriped suit.

"Politics has become a beauty contest," Mrs. Thompson quipped.

The camera focused on the senator: "If I am elected governor, I will propose radically new legislation. Right now the law says you must be legally drunk to be charged with drunk driving. But I say this: Under the new law, if you cause an accident which results in a fatality, and you have *any* trace of alcohol or drugs in your bloodstream—not point one percent the way the current law reads, *but any trace at all*—you will automatically be charged with second-degree manslaughter."

The camera cut away to the crowd of applauding Jaycees.

"Nothing like riding a trend," Mrs. Thompson said.

Matt suddenly had an idea. He stood up.

"Where are you going?" his mother asked.

"I have to check something," he said.

He ran upstairs into his room and pulled out the photocopy of the blood alcohol concentrations. Chris .17; Bobby .06. One phrase kept ringing in his head. *"Any trace at all."*

He went into his mother's room and dialed Lee's

number. It rang twelve times, but no one answered. Lee had told him not to call the police station, but this was important. Matt dialed the station and asked for him.

Seconds later, Lee was on the line. "Hello?"

"Lee, it's Matt."

Don's brother was quiet for a moment. Then he said, "I asked you not to call me here."

"This is important," Matt insisted. "I have to talk to you."

"Later."

"No, now."

"I'm sorry, Matt, I—"

"Listen," Matt cut him off. "I think I know what happened. And if I'm right I think I can prove it too."

Lee coughed and cleared his throat. "Meet me in the parking lot behind Grace Church in twenty minutes." He hung up.

Matt ran downstairs and grabbed the car keys. He was just inches from the door to the garage when his mother said, "Where are you going?"

"I, uh, have to see someone."

"It's about the accident, isn't it?"

"Yes."

His mother sighed. "Just be careful."

He got the car out of the garage and drove to Grace Church. The parking lot was packed with cars belonging to bingo players. Matt couldn't find a place to park, so he sat in the car and let it idle. *Any trace at all,* he thought. The answer had been in front of him ever since he'd driven up to Flathead Mountain and looked at the wreck. He just hadn't put it all together. Until now.

A few minutes later Lee tapped the car window. Matt jumped. He opened the door and Lee got in.

"Drive around the block." Lee crouched in the seat, his knees almost under his chin, his head touching the roof of the car.

"You can move the seat back," Matt said.

"Don't worry about it."

Matt drove out of the lot.

"I don't have much time, Matt. Make it fast."

"First, congratulations on your promotion."

Lee snorted. "I assume Don told you. Thanks. Now what's up?"

"When you came to school the other day," Matt said. "You said that even if someone had a blood alcohol concentration of less than point one it could still affect his driving."

"Uh-huh."

"Then in the parking lot. You told me that a person with an alcohol concentration of point one seven would be so drunk he couldn't walk straight."

"That's right."

"How would a person with point oh six act?"

Lee rubbed his chin and stared at the empty sidewalk. "If he put his mind to it, he could look pretty sober."

"Even if he was under the influence," Matt said.

"Even then."

So that was the answer, Matt thought. No wonder they didn't want him to know. He pulled around the corner and back into the Grace Church parking lot. The streetlights angled into the car, but Matt could barely see Lee's face in the shadows as he said, "You're going to find that figuring it out was the easy part, Matt. The hard part is what comes next. Whatever you do,

promise me you'll think long and hard about the ramifications. Not only how it will affect other people, but
how it will affect you."

"I promise," Matt said.

Lee reached for the door handle, then stopped and
looked at him. "And keep my name out of it."

"Done," said Matt.

Lee got out of the car and walked into the dark.

Matt's next stop was Jason's house. As he drove he
thought about what Lee had said. *"The hard part is
what comes next."* He could see that. But he wasn't
quite there yet.

Jason lived in a small, old gray wooden house near the
railroad station. Matt had never been inside. He'd only
stopped in front with Bobby either to pick Jason up or
drop him off. There was a hedge in front of the house
and a long narrow driveway leading to a separate garage in back. Matt parked and went up the walk to the
porch and rang the bell.

A stocky woman answered the door. She was wearing
a hairnet over pink curlers.

"Is Jason here?" Matt asked.

"Out in the garage," the woman said. "You can go
around the side."

Matt went back down the porch steps and circled
around the house. The garage wasn't much more than a
weather-beaten shack. A dented green Oldsmobile
Ninety-eight was parked in the driveway. As he walked
past the car he noticed the air had that snow smell
again. He looked up and couldn't see any stars. It must
have been pretty cloudy.

A radio was playing inside the garage. He was about
to knock, but stopped. A row of small glass windows

lined the top of the garage door. Standing on his toes, he could see inside.

The garage was lit by a light bulb hanging from a rafter. Old tires leaned against the wall next to a lawn mower and some outdoor furniture. Directly under the light bulb was a motorcycle. A new one. Jason was squatting on the floor beside it, screwing a license plate onto the tail. Now Matt knew his hunch was right.

He reached down and pulled open the garage door. Jason jumped up and turned to face him. For a second they stood in the light and stared at each other.

"Who invited you?" Jason asked.

"You and Bobby wanted to take the girls up to the ski house," Matt told him. "But you couldn't all fit in Bobby's car. Chris had the Blazer, but he was too drunk to drive. So Bobby drove. After the crash, Mr. Stewart didn't want anyone to know that, so he used his influence to change the story. He paid you off with this motorcycle."

"You're out of your mind."

"Then how'd you get it?"

"Saved for it," Jason said.

Matt blinked. That was what Chris had said when Matt had asked him how he'd bought the Blazer. It was bull then and it was bull now.

"You're lying."

"Prove it."

"I will." Matt started to walk back down the driveway.

"And then what?" Jason yelled after him. "You think you'll be a big hero? You think people will look at you and say, 'There goes Matt Thompson, the guy who revealed the truth about how those kids were killed'?"

Matt stopped and looked back.

"Don't you understand?" Jason asked. "Nobody wants to know that. They *want* to think Chris did it. All you're going to do is get that new pool taken away. No one's going to think you're a hero. They're going to think you're a real jerk."

"And you'd let Chris's mother go through the rest of her life thinking it was her son's fault that those kids were killed?" Matt asked.

"It won't make any difference," Jason said.

"We'll see," said Matt, turning toward the street.

"You'll be sorry, Thompson," Jason said behind him.

23

Matt lay in bed that night thinking. The hard part was what happened next, Lee had said. Was he right? What would happen if Matt told what he knew? What *were* the ramifications? Was it losing the swimming pool that had everyone so ticked? Were they really willing to let Mrs. Walsh go through the rest of her life thinking it was Chris who'd gotten those kids killed? It didn't make sense. Why would the police and the guy at the Arco station care about the pool?

THE ACCIDENT

He got out of bed, pulled on his robe, and sat down by the window. A streetlight glowed outside. Chris used to sit on the curb under the light and drink beer. But the cops would come around and hassle him so he took to sitting behind Matt's unit and drinking there. Matt grinned. What a crazy kid.

Then he thought about the cornice and how he'd watched Jason throw himself off it just to prove he belonged. Maybe Karen was right. Matt wasn't a chicken. He simply understood that he didn't have to risk his neck. He pressed his fingertips against the cold window. Jason wasn't so bad. Just a new kid at school trying to make friends. Maybe, Matt thought, he'd been a little hard on him, a little jealous because Bobby liked him. What made Matt think Bobby was his possession? He was free to pick his friends.

But what about the motorcycle in Jason's garage? There had to be more to it. *The hard part is what happens next.* He was sure Bobby had driven the Blazer even though neither Lee nor Jason had said so. But there was still one person who was at the party the night of the accident, but wasn't on Lee's list. The one person who could tell Matt he was right.

It was snowing the next morning. It must have started around dawn because Matt could still see some grass under the thin white blanket. After breakfast he took his junior yearbook and went over to the Walshes'. He knocked on the door and Casey answered, wearing pink pajamas. The Saturday-morning cartoons were blaring on the TV.

"Can I come in for a second?" Matt asked.

Casey stepped away from the door and let him in.

"Your mom home?"

Casey shook her head. Mrs. Walsh was probably at church. Well, that was okay for now. Matt went into the living room and sat down on the couch with the yearbook in his lap. Casey followed him and stood nearby, one eye on the cartoons.

"Listen, Casey," Matt said. "I have to ask you about something serious. About Chris."

Casey's expression didn't change. She kept glancing at the cartoons.

"Casey, listen." Matt tried to get her attention. "Did your mom ever talk to you about the accident? About how Chris died?"

Casey nodded.

"She said the truck crashed, right?" Matt said.

"Kwiss went to Hewwen," Casey said simply.

"Did she ever say anything else about the crash?" Matt asked. "Like who was driving or anything like that?"

Casey shook her head.

"Do you remember the night of the party?" asked Matt. "The last time you saw Chris?"

The TV heroes were zapping the monsters. Matt wasn't sure Casey had heard him. He opened the yearbook. "Look, Casey, I want to show you something." He turned to the pictures of last year's junior class. They were typical class pictures, arranged by homeroom, of everyone jammed together on the bleachers. The short kids sat in front and the tall kids stood in back. One photo per page. He turned to Chris's old homeroom.

Casey looked at the book.

"Can you find Chris?" Matt asked.

She pointed to Chris's picture.

"Casey, the night of the party you stayed in your room," Matt told her. "But you watched from your window. Some kids in front were making noise. Then some other kids came out and got into the truck."

"Kwiss tuck," Casey said.

"Did you see them get into the truck?" Matt asked.

When Casey nodded, Matt felt goose bumps rise on his arms and neck. "Someone got in the driver's seat of Chris's truck. You know, the seat with the steering wheel. Was it Chris?"

Casey thought for a second and then glanced back at the TV. The zapping was loud.

"Casey, listen," Matt urged. "This is super-important. Did Chris get into the driver's seat?"

Still watching the TV, Casey shook her head slowly.

"Look." Matt turned to the page with Bobby's home-room. Bobby was standing in the middle of the last row, about four inches taller than the guys next to him. "Is the person who got into the driver's seat on this page?"

Casey studied the photo. She nodded.

Matt felt his heart beat. His mouth was dry. "Could you point to that person?"

Casey didn't hesitate. Her finger went straight to Bobby.

"You sure he's the one who drove?" Matt asked. "Are you super-sure?"

Casey pointed at Bobby again and nodded.

Matt stood up. "Okay, Casey, thanks." He walked toward the front door. Casey watched him, but kept glancing back at the TV. At the door he waved good-bye. She turned and stared at the set.

As he walked back to his house Matt thought about what had just happened. Thanks to Casey, his suspicions had proved right beyond a doubt. Great. That was the easy part. Now he had to decide what to do. He brushed the snow off his boots and let himself into the house.

"Matt, that you?" his mother called from the kitchen. "Come in here for a second."

Matt pulled off his boots and went into the kitchen. His mother was just putting a big dish of lasagna— homemade for a change—in the oven, preparing a couple of nights' worth of dinners for the next week. She closed the oven door.

"Mr. Stewart just called. He wants to see you as soon as possible." She glanced at the yearbook in his hands. "Do you know what he wants?"

Matt put the book on the kitchen table and sat down. His arms felt heavy. He was starting to feel the effects of lost sleep. "I've got a pretty good idea."

"You found something out, didn't you?" she said.

"Uh-huh."

"Do you want to tell me?"

"Think long and hard about the ramifications," Lee had said. Matt looked up at his mother. "No, Mom, I better wait."

24

Twenty minutes later, Matt sat in his mother's car on the side of Auburn Way. Small, perfect snowflakes fell out of the gray February sky and landed on the windshield. There was no wind and each flake floated peacefully down, hitting the sloping glass and sliding a few inches until it came to a stop.

Matt took a deep breath and began to gnaw on his thumbnail. Bobby's father knew. Jason must have called him. What was Mr. Stewart going to do?

Matt didn't know. The Stewarts lived in a world filled with mansions, chauffeured limousines, and private jets. Maybe they lived by a different set of rules from Matt, or maybe he'd just seen too many episodes of *Dallas.* Either way, Matt was scared.

A small clump of snow broke away from a branch in the tree above him. It hit the windshield with a splash of white. Matt took a deep breath and told himself to get moving.

A few moments later he parked the car in front of the Stewart mansion and got out. He climbed the steps and wiped his shoes. John opened the door and escorted him in.

The den was well lit this time, and empty.

"Mr. Stewart will be with you in a moment," John said, and pulled the door closed. Matt's heart raced, his palms were damp. He took deep breaths to calm himself. This was worse than waiting in the dentist's office to have his teeth drilled.

The seconds dragged into minutes. Matt began to feel calmer. The last time he'd been in the den it had been too dark to see much. Now he noticed two framed photographs on the desk. One, an old black and white, the other a recent color shot.

Matt looked at the black-and-white photo first. It was a shot of three young men and a young woman on a wooden dock on a lake. The young woman had on a bathing cap, the young men were wearing baggy bathing suits. One was Bobby's father and the other was Senator Stewart. He guessed that the young woman was Bobby's philanthropic aunt. But who was the third man? Then he remembered the story Bobby's father had told him about the brother who had died.

The other photo was of Bobby and his two brothers,

also in bathing suits, also standing on a dock. From the turquoise-colored water and the palms in the background, Matt guessed it had been taken in Mexico.

Both photos showed young men who'd died at an early age. Matt wondered if there was any worse tragedy for a brother, a sister, a parent. All the money and cars and vacation houses in the world couldn't protect you. When it came to dying, everyone was equal.

The door opened and Mr. Stewart stepped in. Matt straightened up. Bobby's father looked better than he had the last time Matt had seen him. He was clean shaven and the bags under his eyes weren't so obvious.

He gestured to Matt to sit down on the leather couch. Matt sat at one end, Mr. Stewart at the other.

"So you know," Mr. Stewart said. He didn't sound angry.

"Yes," Matt said.

Mr. Stewart's fingers toyed with the end of his tie. "I guess the thing I don't understand is why you would want to do this to Bobby. You were his closest friend."

Matt felt his heart start to thump again and took another deep breath. "Mr. Stewart, I don't want to hurt anyone. I just want to do what's right. It's wrong to let people think it was Chris's fault when it really wasn't. People have been blaming Chris for things his whole life. Bobby was my best friend, but it's still not fair."

Mr. Stewart placed his hands on his knees and nodded. "I agree with you, Matt. It's not fair. But stop for a moment and look at the bigger picture. My brother is running for governor. He is an honest, hardworking politician who can do a great many things for the people of this state, and he is attempting to unseat a governor who is corrupt, lazy, and incompetent. If my brother becomes governor I can promise you the laws he will enact will result in fewer accidents like the one that killed Bobby."

"But why can't you tell people that Bobby was the driver?" Matt asked. "They'd understand. They wouldn't think that just because Bobby was driving the truck that your brother won't be a good governor."

Mr. Stewart frowned. "You're right, but if it were that simple we never would have gone to these lengths to change the story. If there's one thing I've learned about politics, it's that people's opinions can be easily swayed. Governor Hughes is a desperate and immoral politician. He knows the polls are against him, and he'll do anything to stay in power. If he knew what really happened he would bend the truth to make the Stewart family look like a bunch of wealthy imbeciles who can't control their children. He would make a mockery of my brother's campaign for stiffer DWI laws. Hughes has been governor for a long time and he has the power to sway the media and public opinion in this state. Believe me, Matt, he would use this tragedy against us."

"But isn't it immoral *not* to tell the people the truth?" asked Matt.

"In almost every case, I would say the answer is yes," Mr. Stewart said. "But in this case the good of telling the truth must be weighed against the consequences. The leadership of this state has been corrupt for decades. They have stolen and misused tens of millions of dollars. My brother is not corrupt. He has no reason to steal money, frankly because he already has more than enough."

"But he used his influence to get the chief of police to change his story," Matt said.

"No. My brother knows nothing about this."

Matt blinked. "Then how?"

"I arranged it,"

Matt didn't kno...

toward him. "I'm no...

you, Matt. You're a bri...

idealistic. What I think y...

that politics is a game of t...

'I'll scratch your back if 'd...

scratching is done for pers...

corruption. If it's done for th...

called politics."

"But you want your brother ...

said. "How do I know you're not ju...

me from telling the truth?"

Mr. Stewart smiled. "Matt, I want...

governor because I know he'll be goo...

you're asking me if I think I'll gain from...

being governor then the answer is no. I'll ...

little secret, my friend. Now that gold mini...

to thrive again, one of the first bills my broth...

propose would put a surtax on gold profits. The...

from the surtax will go toward education. A great ...

of that money will come from Stewart mines."

"But that still leaves Mrs. Walsh," Matt told him.
"People have thrown garbage all over her lawn. They
shot out one of her windows. They call her names in
town. She has to move away because of this. But wher-
ever she goes she's still going to have to go through the
rest of her life thinking her son was driving."

Mr. Stewart pressed his fingers against his forehead.
"Matt, I'm going to tell you something now that you
must swear you will never repeat to anyone, not your
mother, not anyone. Can you swear that to me?"

Matt nodded.

"Angelica Walsh knows who was driving," Mr. Stew-

...ne knew the day after the accident. ...ale and she's telling people that she's ...ne, but she isn't. She's moving to Seat- ...private school there that specializes in ...ldren with learning disabilities. It's very ...nd very good. Do I have to explain any

...ook his head, stunned.

...w this must be difficult for you," Bobby's father ...ut try to think of this in terms of doing the most ...or the most number of people. The school will get ...w pool. Angelica Walsh will be able to provide a ...d education for her daughter. The state will get an ...nest government"—he paused for a second—"is ...here something you want?"

"Me? No."

"I didn't think there would be," Mr. Stewart said. He gazed at the photos on the desk for a moment. "There's something else I want you to know. If you really, truly feel compelled to tell the world the truth, I won't stop you. The high school will still get its pool and Angelica Walsh's daughter will still get her education. And who knows, my brother may even be elected governor in spite of it. All I ask is that you tell me now so I can warn him."

Matt rubbed the leather armrest with his fingers, and weighed what Mr. Stewart had said. If Mrs. Walsh knew . . . if she'd agreed to change the story, then who was he to disagree? Even she knew Jason was right—people wanted to believe Chris was driving the night of the accident. It fit their expectations. Telling them the truth wouldn't make them feel better, it would make them feel worse. The high school would still get its pool, but the memory of Bobby would be tainted, and

Hughes and his cronies might have another four years to steal from the state.

Matt looked at Mr. Stewart. It was like that day on the cornice, with Bobby waiting in the snow below. What was right? If Bobby could have promised him he'd land without getting hurt, he would have jumped. Now Mr. Stewart was making that promise.

"I'm not going to tell," Matt said.

Bobby's father nodded. "I'm grateful to you for that."

A few minutes later, Matt and Mr. Stewart walked down the steps in front of the mansion and across the snowy driveway to Matt's car. After Matt got in, Mr. Stewart leaned into the window. Snowflakes were collecting on his shoulders and head. "Matt, there's one thing I still can't understand. Bobby drove that road hundreds of times. He knew it like the back of his hand."

"But it wasn't his car," Matt said. "And there were a lot of kids in the truck . . . and he did have alcohol in his blood."

Mr. Stewart looked grim. Matt started to put the key in the ignition.

"Wait, Matt," Mr. Stewart said. "I know you tracked this mystery down because you were a loyal friend, both to Bobby and Chris Walsh. You've shown a great deal of integrity and a desire to know the truth. I know you won't accept anything from me now, but maybe someday after college when it's time for you to start out on your own . . . Well, if you ever want to join one of the Stewart concerns, we'd be glad to have you."

Matt gave him an uneasy look and Mr. Stewart smiled. "Oh, no, Matt. We wouldn't be doing you a favor. You'd be doing one for us."

167

From the Stewarts', Matt drove straight to Karen's house. He rang the doorbell.

Karen pulled back the curtain on the window next to the door. "Go away." She let the curtain fall.

"Wait. This is important." Matt felt like an idiot talking to a door, but he had no choice.

"Not to me it's not."

"Karen, please. At least open the door and let me talk to you. I promise I won't come in . . . Karen?" He heard music. She'd turned on the stereo to drown him out.

"Damn it, Karen!" He banged on the door with his fist, but the music played on. He pressed the doorbell again and kept his finger on the button for five minutes. Finally, he heard the music stop.

"If you don't leave right now, I'm going to call the police," Karen threatened.

Matt looked down and saw the mail slot. He kneeled and pulled it open. He could see Karen's knees. "It's over, Karen. The whole accident thing is finished. I know you won't believe me, so tell me what I have to do to prove it to you."

A second later he saw Karen's eyes through the mail slot. "Why is it over?"

"Because it is."

"You found out what happened?"

"Bobby . . ." Matt suddenly stopped. How could he tell her? He couldn't tell anyone. If he was going to go along with the lie, then he had to become part of it.

"What, Matt?"

His elation drained away. How could he lie to her? But how could he risk telling her the truth? *The hard part is what comes next.* Now he realized what Lee had meant.

Karen pulled open the door. She looked concerned. "Are you okay?"

"Yeah." Matt nodded slowly.

"Tell me what happened. I'm dying to know."

Matt tasted bile. "Chris was driving. Everything else was . . . a figment of my imagination."

He spent the afternoon with Karen. After their talk at the door, they didn't speak about the accident once. Matt pretended the reason he was so bummed out was because he'd been wrong.

It was dinnertime when he got home.

"Where have you been?" his mother asked.

"I'm sorry, Mom," Matt said. "It took longer than I thought."

Peter was sitting at the kitchen table with his Walkman on, playing air-drums with a fork and spoon. He turned down the volume.

"You bring the car back?" he asked.

"No, I left it," Matt said.

Peter twisted around in his chair and yelled to Mrs. Thompson. "Can we go after dinner, Mom? The stores are open late on Saturdays. Can we?"

"Where are you going?" Matt asked.

"Grandpa sent the check," Peter said. "I'm getting a set of drums."

"Oh, great." Matt sighed.

Mrs. Thompson came around the counter with two dishes of lasagna and set them down on the table. Peter and Matt started to eat.

Matt's mother watched him. "How did it go?" she asked.

"Okay," Matt said, scooping lasagna onto his fork.

"That's it? Just okay?"

"Yeah."

"Do you feel better about it now?" she asked.

"A little." Matt took another bite and avoided her gaze. He knew she wasn't satisfied with his reply. For a moment he wished he'd never found out the truth. But now that he had, he was just going to live with it.

Epilogue

25

That fall Matt and Karen went to college in Boston and saw each other as often as their schedules would allow. On election night they sat up together and watched the news until it was announced that Senator William Stewart had been elected governor in their state's contest.

The following day, Matt told Karen the truth about the accident. She listened quietly, then said that she would have done the same thing.

"But you're not the one who has to live with it," Matt said.

At the end of their freshman year they returned to Highland Hills to work for the summer. By then a young woman with a baby had moved into the Walshes' old unit. The new pool at the high school was finished, and Governor Stewart was busy throwing out Hughes's old cronies and revamping the state's laws. The courts had declared the manslaughter law unconstitutional, but Bobby's uncle was able to stiffen the DWI laws and increase the amount of money available for drug and alcohol prevention programs. Everyone thought he was doing a fine job.

On his first evening home, Matt called Lee Washington and asked if he could come over and speak to him.

The address Lee gave him was for an apartment complex in town. Matt climbed the stairs and rang the bell. He smelled pizza. Don's brother opened the door.

"Matt, how are you?" Lee held out his hand.

Matt shook it. "Pretty good. And you?"

"Fine. Come on in. I just ordered a pizza. Hope you like mushroom and sausage."

Matt stepped into the apartment. Lee had set up a card table in front of the television. He brought in an extra chair, put the pizza box on the table, and pulled out a couple of slices. They were just about to sit down when Lee snapped his fingers.

"Beer, Matt?"

"Sure, but I'm a minor," Matt said.

"Oh, yeah, I forgot." Lee chuckled. He went into the kitchen and got a Coors and a can of Coke. "I'm still asked to give lectures about drunk driving at high schools and colleges. You'd think I'd be more careful about who I offered beer to."

Matt laughed and popped the top of the Coke.

"So what are your plans for the summer?" Lee asked.

"Guess I'll get a job," Matt said. "My mom says she knows this lawyer who needs a gofer."

"How come you're not a lifeguard at the municipal pool with Don?" Lee asked. "He told me a bunch of guys from the team got jobs there for the summer."

Matt shrugged. He had hardly spoken to anyone from school since they'd all left for college. Knowing what he knew, it was hard to face them. Don had written him a letter from the State College of Criminology, but Matt hadn't written back.

They bit into their slices. Lee asked him about his year at BU, then reminisced a little about his own college career. Matt found it hard to relax. He had too much on his mind.

"I've thought a lot about the decision you made," Lee said finally. "We never really had a chance to talk about it."

Matt swallowed. "You dropped off the blood alcohol concentrations, right?"

Lee nodded. "I knew what had happened, but I wasn't in a position to do anything about it. If I'd blown the whistle on the chief of police, the department would have run me out of town on a rail. I'd probably never be able to get a job in law enforcement again. And to tell you the truth, Matt, I couldn't decide what the right thing to do was either."

"Why did you pick me?"

"You wanted to know," Lee said. "And maybe I hoped you'd do what I couldn't do."

Matt nodded. "That's why I'm here tonight, Lee. I've changed my mind."

175

Don's brother leaned back in his chair and wiped his lips with a paper napkin. "I had a feeling."

"I wanted to warn you," Matt said.

"I appreciate that."

"What do you think will happen?"

"Nothing," Lee said.

"Nothing?" Matt scowled.

Lee picked up another slice of pizza. "I'll tell you a funny story, Matt. After it became obvious that you'd made your decision, it never stopped bothering me. Even after they made me a detective I felt like I hadn't earned it, they'd just given it to me to keep me quiet. Finally, last November, after the election, I had a talk with the district attorney."

"What happened?" Matt asked.

"Well, I presented the evidence to him and outlined the whole story just like I'd do in any criminal case. When I was finished he said he appreciated what I had to say, but he couldn't prosecute."

"Why not?"

"Because no one was hurt," Lee said. "No one in public office accepted a bribe. No one was the victim of a crime."

"But the mayor and police chief knew Bobby was the driver," Matt said.

Lee bit into his slice and chewed it. "Did it ever occur to you that the real poison, the real sickness, was Hughes? That if he hadn't been such an immoral, dirty politician Mr. Stewart never would have had to cover up Bobby's role in the accident? I know that doesn't excuse him. In a purely ethical sense I agree that what he did was wrong, but look at the outcome. Hughes is out and Governor Stewart is in and good things are

176

happening. By not speaking out, you helped the people of this state."

"So what will happen now if I tell the truth?" Matt asked.

"The papers will have a good time with it. It'll be embarrassing for the mayor and the chief and the Stewarts, but they'll insist they did the right thing and the public will basically agree with them. We already know the DA won't prosecute. It'll probably be a big deal for about two weeks and then everyone will forget about it."

"You think I'd be wasting my time?" Matt asked.

"Oh, no, I didn't mean to imply that at all," Lee said. "You have to do what you think is right."

Matt thought about the consequences while he finished his slice. It might not change things for anyone else, but it would change something for him. He wouldn't have to live with the lie anymore. He stood up.

"Gotta run?" Lee asked.

"I've got some calls to make."

Lee smiled and patted him on the back. "You're a brave kid, Matt."

"Sometimes I think I wasn't when I should have been."

"You were. You did the right thing then, and you're probably doing the right thing now."

Out on the street, Matt stopped at a pay phone to make two calls. The first was to Karen, to ask her to go to a movie that night. The second was to the newspaper.

"*Highland Reporter*," a familiar-sounding voice answered.

"Marvin?"

"Yeah, who's this?"

"Matt Thompson."

"Hey, Matt, how're you doing?"

"Okay. Are you a reporter?"

"Naw, I'm just interning for the summer, answering phones and covering little league. Junk like that."

"So how's it going?"

"Totally boring. You can't believe how dead this town is. You could print all the news on a postage stamp."

Matt chuckled. Same old Marvin. "Listen, get a piece of paper, I think I've got something for you."

"Oh, yeah? Something good?"

"Yeah," Matt said. "Something good."

About the Author

Todd Strasser has written many books for young readers, including *Friends Till the End* and *Rock 'n' Roll Nights*, both named American Library Association Best Books for Young Adults. Among Strasser's other novels are *Angel Dust Blues, A Very Touchy Subject*, and *Wildlife.*

The author lives in New York City with his wife and children.